A Five-Star Family Reunion

Just in time for Christmas!

The Pearson family promised their late mother that, no matter what, they would *always* spend Christmas together. However, it has been three years and their special tradition is almost lost and forgotten...

Chiara has been traveling the world, but she's running out of money and needs help to get home! Meanwhile, Marco has been busy expanding the family hotel business in Europe, and *unexpectedly* expanding the family, too. Having insisted his children make it back by Christmas Eve, Joshua has been preparing their Vermont cabin, until the arrival of his beautiful neighbor puts a wrench in the works...

Whatever it takes, the Pearson family *will* spend Christmas together this year!

Find out more in
Chiara and Evan's story
Wearing His Ring till Christmas
by Nina Singh

Available now!

Look out for
Marco and Eleanora's story
One-Night Baby to Christmas Proposal
by Susan Meier

and

Joshua and Rebecca's story
Christmas with His Ballerina
by Jessica Gilmore

Coming next month!

Dear Reader,

I've always had a rather robust case of wanderlust. It is precisely this yearning that motivates Chiara Pearson to travel to as many places as she can, as a tribute to the loving parent she lost much too young. Only, Chiara's wanderlust finds herself far from home with no way to return and she's promised her family she'll be there for a long-awaited Christmas together.

Then a chance encounter with one of the world's most successful tech pioneers offers her an opportunity to resolve her predicament. Evan Kim needs a temporary fake fiancée for a business deal and Chiara would fit the role perfectly. In return, he promises to get her back to the United States by Christmas and he'll take her to several locations she's always wanted to visit. It all seems so simple and so convenient. But it doesn't take long for Chiara and Evan to start feeling emotions for each other that are all too real, and they so inconveniently begin to fall in love.

This story was such a pleasure to write, as it also gave me the privilege of working with two fellow authors I so admire, Susan Meier and Jessica Gilmore.

I hope you enjoy Chiara and Evan's story.

Nina Singh

Wearing His Ring till Christmas

—

Nina Singh

Special thanks and acknowledgment are given to Nina Singh for
her contribution to A Five-Star Family Reunion miniseries.

Recycling programs
for this product may
not exist in your area.

ISBN-13: 978-1-335-73684-0

Wearing His Ring till Christmas

Copyright © 2022 by Harlequin Enterprises ULC

For questions and comments about the quality of this book,
please contact us at CustomerService@Harlequin.com.

Harlequin Enterprises ULC
22 Adelaide St. West, 41st Floor
Toronto, Ontario M5H 4E3, Canada
www.Harlequin.com

Printed in U.S.A.

Nina Singh lives just outside Boston, Massachusetts, with her husband, children and a very rambunctious Yorkie. After several years in the corporate world, she finally followed the advice of family and friends to "give the writing a go, already." She's oh-so-happy she did. When not at her keyboard, she likes to spend time on the tennis court or golf course. Or immersed in a good read.

Books by Nina Singh

Harlequin Romance

How to Make a Wedding

From Tropical Fling to Forever

Destination Brides

Swept Away by the Venetian Millionaire

Captivated by the Millionaire
Their Festive Island Escape
Her Billionaire Protector
Spanish Tycoon's Convenient Bride
Her Inconvenient Christmas Reunion
From Wedding Fling to Baby Surprise
Around the World with the Millionaire
Whisked into the Billionaire's World

Visit the Author Profile page
at Harlequin.com.

To all my fellow wanderers out there.
Keep roaming and exploring.

Praise for
Nina Singh

"A captivating holiday adventure!
Their Festive Island Escape by Nina Singh is
a twist on an enemies-to-lovers trope and is
sure to delight. I recommend this book to anyone....
It's fun, it's touching and it's satisfying."

—*Goodreads*

CHAPTER ONE

SHE HAD TO get her act together already. Chiara Pearson plopped down on the bed she'd made—and if that wasn't a metaphor, she didn't know what was—then slid her cell phone into her maid uniform pocket. Lately, as much as she loved him, speaking with her dad left her apprehensive and anxious afterward.

The call she'd just disconnected had been no different.

Of course, it was her own fault. No fault of Joshua Pearson's whatsoever that their long-distance conversations recently left her shaky and guilt ridden. After all, she was the one lying to her own parent. Well, perhaps lying was a bit harsh. She was merely fibbing a bit, telling the old man what he wanted to hear. And that would be that Chiara was all set to travel in a few weeks to be with him and her brother at Christmas. But the truth was she had no idea how she might pull that off.

She was beyond broke. Barely covering the expense of living in Bali. Luckily, her job at the Garden Beach Hotel afforded her a couple meals throughout the day. Anything left over after the buffet-style meals served to guests was fair game once the event was over. She refused to think of them as leftover scraps. Because that thought was just too demeaning. Not that she could think of a better way to describe what it was.

But she had even less clue about how to break the news to her parent that she had little to no money with which to pay for a trip home. Her father would give her more money, no question about it. He wouldn't even hesitate. If it weren't for her pride, she'd be tempted to ask him to do just that.

He would be absolutely devastated if she broke her word about being there for Christmas this year.

Her phone vibrated in her pocket and Chiara hesitated to pull it out to see who the caller might be. If it was Dad calling her back for some reason, she might very well break down and admit her failings, admit that she'd lied to him about how well she was doing and how solvent she was.

Guilt had her hesitation ending just before the call went to voice mail.

With a sigh, she pulled the device out to look at the screen. Not her father, thank goodness. But only a slightly better scenario that the caller happened to be her brother, Marco. She clicked the answer icon.

"Hey, sis. Been trying to call you. Where've you been?"

Despite the situation, Chiara couldn't help the warm affection that spread through her chest. Marco and her father were the only immediate family she had now, and she cherished them. As she did the memory of her mother. They'd always been a very close unit. One that was now irreparably fractured.

"Hey yourself," she replied. "I was on the phone with Pa. You know how long those calls can be." Their father was definitely not the strong, silent type when it came to conversations with his kids.

Marco chuckled. "Let me guess. He wanted to go over all the Christmas plans. Over and over and over again."

Chiara tried to squelch down the panic bubbling through her chest at the mention of Christmas. Time to come clean.

But Marco didn't give her a chance. Before she'd taken her next breath, he continued speaking. And his words crumbled her already fragile resolve. "I've never seen him so excited for the holidays, sis. Keeps talking about how we'll finally all be together again."

Perhaps not all of us, Chiara thought, the sting of tears behind her eyes. "He does?"

"Oh, yeah." He paused a beat. "And if I'm being honest, I have to admit to being pretty excited myself. It has been a while, hasn't it?"

Something twisted in the area around her chest. Now her brother was talking up the holiday season. As if hearing Dad's hearty excitement earlier wasn't bad enough. Of course, she wanted to be with them in December. But fate didn't seem to be on her side these days.

Not that she wouldn't make the same decisions all over again if given the chance. How could she have turned down a friend who needed her money more than she did?

"Um… I have to go Marco. Rooms to clean and all that."

"I understand," he answered. Chiara could see the smile he'd spoken through clearly in her mind's eye. "Call me later."

"I will." She'd have to. After she'd built up enough courage through the day, she'd have to call her brother and let him know once and for all that she most likely wouldn't be able to make it back to the States for the holidays, after all. Despite all her assurances and promises earlier in the year that she wouldn't miss it for the world.

Telling Marco could serve as a practice run for the dreaded conversation she would have to have with her father. It would give her a nice preview of the lecture she'd receive. About how she was too spontaneous for her own good. Or how she never thought things through about what her decisions would mean long-term.

Chiara walked over to the glass doors of the balcony to stare at the misty gray sky outside. Bali was such a gorgeous location. Full of culture and national spirit. But Decembers were often rainy and wet most days. Today was no exception. And it fit her mood perfectly.

She couldn't dwell on her melancholy right now. There was a full day's worth of work that awaited her. The last thing she needed was to jeopardize her job. Cleaning rooms at a luxurious beachside hotel wasn't the most glamorous of duties. But she desperately needed the money. Especially now that she'd given away the money Papa had sent her. The savings she'd been putting away painstakingly for the past several weeks simply wouldn't be enough to cover what she needed.

What in the world was she going to do?

Giving her head a shake, she turned away from the view and went to her utility cart. She had plenty of time to fret over her predicament as she scrubbed and wiped for the next several hours.

Not that she had any hope of coming up with any kind of solution.

Evan Kim stared at the crisp white envelope he held in his hands and bit out a curse. He didn't need to open it to know what it was. An invitation to the wedding of the century. As far as those in his former circle were concerned, anyway. Especially his parents.

That thought made him wince.

Not that he wasn't happy for Louis. He really was. His friend was one of the most genuine and generous people Evan knew. He deserved all the good fortune the universe seemed to be bestowing upon him at the moment.

No, the issue Evan had about his friend's upcoming nuptials had nothing to do with the groom nor the bride—a lovely woman who was currently taking the music world by storm as a classical violinist.

The problem Evan had was completely about the wedding itself, as well as the ceremony. And all those who would be in attendance. Every instinct he possessed screamed at him to send his regrets.

But that would be the coward's way out. Evan

had many faults. But being a coward was certainly not one of them.

Of course, he wouldn't send his regrets. Besides, he had too much respect for Louis to be a no-show at the man's wedding. They'd been as close as brothers growing up. It was bad enough Evan had missed the weeklong excursions in Hong Kong for the bachelor party activities. No, Evan would go of course. And he'd endure the pain and awkwardness that would ensue as soon as he came across his parents.

Evan sighed and tossed the envelope onto the still-unmade bed. Walking over to the window overlooking the water, he ran a frustrated hand through the hair at his crown.

To make matters worse, he'd be attending the wedding sans a plus-one. His mother was sure to comment on that. Right after she reminded him what a disappointment he was as a son. His father would simply nod in agreement.

Most peoples' parents would have been impressed with him as a son. But not his.

All his success. Everything he'd accomplished on his own. None of it mattered as far as his mother and father were concerned. All they cared about was that he'd turned away from the family business. Hence, he'd turned away from *them*.

Same story for years now. One would think Evan would be past the point of having any of it affect him. But it wasn't in his nature to be comfortable with failure. And when it came to his parents, he'd indeed failed them. Apparently, nothing he did would ever be enough. In his parents eyes, his betrayal was absolute because he'd turned down the family business. The ultimate sin for the only Kim heir.

Well, it wouldn't do him any good to dwell on it now. He had a lot to deal with at the moment. He'd rushed back to Bali for a technology convention being held right here in the hotel he called home. The convention would finally grant him the opportunity to meet with the Italian AI company he'd been courting for several months now. Between that and the latest rollout of his gaming app, he had plenty on his plate without drama from the past intruding on his focus.

He strode to the corner desk and reached for his laptop just as the ding of a direct message appeared on the screen. His assistant back in the US with an ominous question.

Have you been online yet today?

He had not. And he could think of only one reason Emily might be asking. Some tawdry website had done yet another hit piece on him. He hammered out a quick reply before calling up a browser to check.

Yep. Bingo.

He was trending. Again. For all the wrong reasons. Nothing to do with the popular game app he'd developed or any of his latest investments. No. Someone had found and posted several photos of Evan partying on a yacht surrounded by scantily clad laughing women.

The film festival he'd attended last month. He'd just been trying to let off some steam after weeks of tense negotiations around a new development deal. Clearly, he should have been more careful about the wayward cell phone camera that had captured in him in full party mode.

Evan bit out another curse and slammed the laptop cover closed. The timing couldn't have been worse. He had to convince the Italian businessmen tomorrow that he was a serious and competent professional who would do well on their board. But his reputation as a ruckus-raising partier seemed to follow him and pop up at the most inopportune times.

His cell phone vibrated with a call. Emily.

"Please tell me you're calling to say you've already rolled out some damage control."

"I'm working on it."

"Isn't there some feel-good story we can have

our media team push to replace some of these hashtags?"

"Hmm. Unfortunately not. But there does seem to be a developing story about that one influencer and her rocker ex-husband fighting about a custody dispute."

Evan scoffed. "Marriage. What a scam, right?" The very idea of matrimony made Evan shudder. His own parents were still together but Evan couldn't recall a time he'd witnessed any kind of display of affection between them.

Emily didn't respond to that. Instead, Evan heard a deep sigh from the other end of the line. "I'm not calling about the photos, boss. I'm afraid I have some more bad news."

Evan pinched the bridge of his nose. "Let me hear it."

"The Italian translator just canceled. Some type of family emergency."

Great. Just great. Was anything going to go right today? Anything at all? This technology convention in Bali was Evan's best chance to meet face-to-face with Roma AI and convince them he was a sure investment. Now he wouldn't even be able to communicate effectively.

"Thanks for the update, Em," he replied before disconnecting.

He needed to get some air.

Not bothering with a jacket, he strode to the

door and rode the elevator from the penthouse level to the first floor. He'd seen a beachside restaurant/bar adjacent to the hotel on his way in earlier this afternoon and he hadn't eaten all day.

A heady cocktail and the view of the sunset over the water might help to clear out some of the frustration currently riding through his system. He just needed to step back and gather his thoughts.

Something had to go his way tonight.

Maybe she could pick up an extra shift or two. Chiara grunted as soon as the thought occurred to her. A measly added shift wasn't going to come close to covering her airfare back to the States. She didn't regret giving Jess the money. Of course not. The woman had needed it much more than she did. But it had brought her to this current precarious position.

There was nothing for it. Only two choices. Chiara had to either figure out a way to get the money or she had to come clean to her dad and tell him she wasn't going to make it, after all. And break his heart in the process. The thought of that crushed her. She'd made him a promise. The burn of fresh tears stung her eyes, but she refused to let them fall. She was done feeling sorry for herself.

Hanging up her uniform in one of the closets in the housekeeping quarters, she undid her ponytail and let her hair fall loose. It felt good to be in her own clothes. Though still desperate for some kind of solution, at least she felt a little better.

Now all she needed was a meal and refreshing swim. Not necessarily in that order. She always kept a spare swimsuit in her tote bag. Being in the water never failed to help soothe her nerves. If only temporarily.

Chiara wasted little time making her way to the hotel's beachside restaurant and bar. Clive, the bartender on call this time of day, was one of her favorites. He'd been one of the first people she'd met when she arrived in Bali two months ago and landed the housekeeping job at the hotel. He was generous with a smile, and he was always good for a laugh.

The complimentary meal he usually sent her way helped, too.

But when she got to the bar area, Clive looked as flustered and harried as she felt. The place was packed. Every table was full, every stool occupied.

"Some kind of technology convention," Clive explained when she approached him.

"Can I help?" So much for relaxing for a few

minutes. But the bar staff was clearly swamped. And she still harbored some nervous energy she could work off.

"You're an angel for offering." He handed her a tray. "Here. Table fourteen. I appreciate it."

Dropping her tote bag behind the bar, Chiara took the loaded tray and turned on her heel.

Then slammed into what had to be a solid wall. "Oh!"

One of the bottles slid off the tray and she waited for the inevitable spray of cold beer to splash her lower legs and shoes. But it never came.

It took a minute for her to get her bearings. The object she'd collided with wasn't a wall at all. It was a man. And said man was currently stabilizing her with one hand on her upper arm even as he'd caught the falling bottle with the other. Some impressive reflexes. She started to tell him so and stopped short. Even in her frazzled state, her breath caught when she looked up at him.

For a fraction of a second, Chiara thought she must be imagining just how handsome he was. He sported just a hint of a five o'clock shadow over a strong jawline. Soulful dark eyes a woman could easily lose herself in. Jet-black hair the color of midnight. He looked like he could have stepped out of an ad for a yacht or cologne.

And her skin tingled where he still touched her.

Somehow, Evan managed to catch the frosty beer bottle before it hit the ground, only a minimal amount of liquid escaping the narrow mouth and hitting the sand by his feet. And he didn't know exactly what the young woman had muttered in her alarm but his rudimentary knowledge of the language told him it was most definitely Italian.

Huh. Maybe his luck was about to change, after all.

A pair of sapphire-blue eyes blinked up at him in clear gratitude. "Uh, thanks."

He felt as if someone had just landed a gut punch when his gaze landed on her face. She was stunning in a way he'd be hard-pressed to describe. Tanned skin, long wavy hair that fell past her shoulders. Her eyes reminded him of the color of morning sky over an ocean.

Since when had he become so poetic?

"I'm so terribly sorry," she said, straightening and balancing the tray. "I guess I wasn't watching where I was going. I'm a little distracted," she added almost as an afterthought, as if she were talking to herself more than to him.

It took Evan a moment to find his voice. "My fault," he finally managed. "I was staring at my phone. Walking and scrolling. Bad combo." A habit he typically abhorred when he witnessed it in others. But he'd been checking that blasted hashtag to see if he was still trending in the top-twenty topics.

She answered him with a small smile. "We all do it."

The accent clearly said American. Maybe he'd simply been hearing what he wanted to hear when he thought she'd spoken Italian earlier.

Several moments passed in awkward silence. For the life of him, Evan couldn't come up with a single word to say. When was the last time that had ever happened to him?

Never. The answer was never.

Somehow this waitress had rendered him dumbstruck. Finally, she lifted the tray ever so slightly. "Well, I should deliver these."

"Of course," he said, stepping out of her way.

By the time he'd found an empty stool at the bar and sat down, she'd delivered her load and come back for more. Evan ordered the nightly special and a strong brandy. All thoughts of gossip websites and AI meetings seemed to have slipped his mind. His focus remained squarely on the pretty waitress who quickly and efficiently served the crowded bar and cleaned and wiped tables in between orders.

He could hardly take his eyes off her.

CHAPTER TWO

AN HOUR LATER, the crowd in the bar was finally starting to thin out. Evan realized with surprise that he'd barely touched his food, despite having found it delicious. And his drink remained full in his glass. He'd slipped into hyper-focus mode at some point. It must have happened when he'd finally managed to pull his gaze away from the pretty waitress he'd almost barreled over upon arrival. In front of him on the table sat a napkin scribbled full with notes and ideas, all the things he wanted to go over with at the meeting tomorrow night. If he could somehow get past the language barrier.

His eye automatically roamed the bar area until he found her. She'd finally sat down at one of the smaller tables, holding a glass of wine and picking at a plate of food. Had he or had he not heard her utter an Italian word earlier?

Only one way to find out.

Hah. He wasn't fooling himself. It was an

excuse to go talk to her. He did owe her a real apology, after all. He'd been practically tongue-tied when he'd tried to say sorry before. Rising out of his chair, he grabbed his drink and made his way over to where she sat.

His pulse quickened and he felt his mouth go dry. He was actually nervous! How utterly surprising. He'd never had any sort of problem approaching women before. Though it didn't happen often—usually *they* approached *him*.

Halfway to his destination, she suddenly looked up. Evan's heart skipped a beat as their eyes caught. Too late to back out now. She was watching him. Her lips curved into a small smile. He was going to go ahead and take that as an invitation.

"Hello again," he said when he reached her table, then immediately cringed at his words.

That's it, fella. Dazzle her with some charming and witty conversation-opener.

How lame could he be?

"Hi."

"I just wanted to come over and offer another apology. I'm so sorry that I almost knocked you over."

The smile widened. "That's very nice of you. But not necessary. You did catch my fall, after all. Plus, I wasn't paying attention to where I was headed. Like you, I was a little distracted myself."

A tightness settled over her face as she made the admission.

"Oh?" There was clearly a story there. Why did he want to hear about it so badly? It shocked him how curious he was about her given that he'd just laid eyes on the woman and any story she might have was really none of his business.

"Do you want to talk about it?" Again. Very original line. *Not.*

She gave a small shake of her head. "I wouldn't want to bore you."

"Please, you'd be taking my mind off my own woes." Woes? Had he really just said he had woes? Why was he acting so uncharacteristically around this woman?

She shrugged. "Sure. Why not?"

He clasped a hand to his chest in mock horror. "Your lack of enthusiasm is downright wounding."

She chuckled. "I'm sorry. What I meant to say was I'd be delighted and could use the company."

He returned her smile. "That's so much better. Thanks."

"You're welcome."

Pointing at her, Evan remarked. "You don't

have a name tag." Unlike the other servers, she wasn't wearing one.

"That's because I'm not technically here."

"I have quite the imagination, then."

She chuckled at that. "I only came down after my cleaning shift for a bite to eat. But I saw they needed help. I'm Chiara."

"Evan. You work here at the hotel?"

She nodded.

"So, Chiara. Do you live here in Bali, then?"

She shook her head in answer. "Well, yes. And no. I'm here temporarily but long-term."

"I see. Business or pleasure?"

"Both, I guess. I'm here mainly to sightsee but working to support my travel habit."

He nodded. "That can be an expensive habit."

"You would know firsthand, I'm guessing."

"I do get around. You're right. Bali is my long-term home at the moment. I'm here now for this technology convention. But more for an important meeting it's taken me weeks to set up. Only it might be a bust now."

She took a sip of her wine. "How so?"

"I need a translator but the one I hired canceled at the last minute. So now I don't know how much I'm going to be able to even get across to the folks I'll be meeting with."

"I'm sorry to hear that."

He leaned toward. "I have a confession I should make to you."

Her eyes grew wide. "A confession?"

"That's right. For a second back there, when we ran into each other, I thought I heard you say something in Italian."

A rosy blush spread across her cheeks. "Oh, I do that sometimes. Hopefully, no one around here understands Italian. It wasn't a very nice term I called out."

So he'd been right. Evan resisted the urge to pump his fist in the air in triumph. Maybe this dreadful day might end in a stroke of luck. "You're not gonna believe this, Chiara, but you might be the answer to all my current problems." Realizing how close those words came to sounding like a cheesy pickup line, he immediately added, "In a completely professional way."

She blinked at him. "How so?"

"The translator I need happens to be for Italian. Any chance you're free tomorrow evening? Of course, you'll be comp—"

She held up her hands before he could go any further. "Whoa, let's slow down a bit here. I don't claim to be anywhere near fluent."

"Can you carry a conversation?"

She shrugged. "I suppose so. My mom spoke Italian to me and my brother sparingly growing up. We were much more comfortable with

English. And I certainly don't know any technical terms. Probably wouldn't know those in English for that matter."

He chuckled. "Leave that part up to me. Coding and AI is universal. I need you for the conversational pieces."

She crossed her arms in front of her chest. "I don't know…"

That wasn't a *no*.

"Where is this meeting to be held exactly?" she asked, eyeing him.

"Right here in the hotel. Your territory. A dinner meeting."

"I could definitely use the funds," she said under her breath, as if thinking out loud. Evan didn't the think the comment was meant for him. "I'm supposed to travel back to the States to spend Christmas in Vermont with my brother and father. Only I'm a little short on funds at the moment."

"If your father wants you there badly enough, won't he just give you the funds?"

She ducked her head with a sheepish motion. "He already did. I gave it away. I can't bring myself to ask for more."

"You gave it away?"

She nodded. "To one of the boarders at the hostel I've been staying at. She was here on a backpacking trip, too. Came to Bali after her boyfriend proposed to her because she wasn't sure about saying yes. Needed time away from him to process and make a decision."

"I see."

"Anyway, the boyfriend was in a horrible motorcycle accident a couple of weeks ago. The scare told her everything she needed to know about how much she loved him. She was frantic, had to get back to the States right away."

"That's terrible. But what does that have to do with you giving away your—" Evan didn't have to finish the question as the answer came to him. This lovely person sitting before him had given away her travel money to someone she'd just met. "You paid for her to go back to the States, didn't you? To go back to her boyfriend?"

She nodded slowly. "How could I not?"

Many people would not have. In fact, most wouldn't.

Chiara released a heavy sigh. "You know what? Why not? I'll do it."

Evan felt a surge of relief flow through him along with something else he didn't want to examine too closely. He couldn't deny, language assistance aside, the fact that he'd be seeing her again held its own appeal.

He leaned closer to her over the table. "Then name your price, Miss Pearson."

* * *

How in the world had she ended up here?

I hope that spontaneity trait of yours doesn't get you in trouble one day. Her father's voice echoed in her head.

Her mother's followed immediately behind, however. *Don't waste any opportunity, Chiara. You will most often live to regret it.*

Chiara sighed. She'd long ago accepted the warring voices in her head borne of both parents' warnings over the years. Her mother's usually won out, for better or worse. It convinced her to make the most of her life in a way that her mother couldn't.

Besides, the question was more of a figurative one. Because the answer was clear. She was in this predicament because she needed the extra cash. It wouldn't cover the full cost of travel back to the States. But it was going to make a good dent. She must have lowballed herself when Evan had asked her price because he'd scoffed at the number, then said he'd pay three times the amount.

Chiara smoothed a hand down her midriff and studied herself in the mirror. Not bad for a girl who'd worked eighteen out of the past twenty-four hours. The silk red dress she'd borrowed from one of the lounge singers luckily fit her well and flattered her curves in all the right ways, if she did say so herself.

So she looked all right, she supposed. But was she really about to play translator for an international businessman she'd literally met the day before? What if she couldn't pull it off?

An ill-formed whistling sound echoed through the air behind her. Nuri bounced into the room and took her shoulders from behind.

"You look fabulous, Chi! Those businessmen we'll be unable to tear their eyes off you."

Chiara smiled at her friend in the mirror. "Never mind that. I just hope they understand me. It's been a decade since I had a conversation in Italian. And that was a very basic one talking about the weather with my mom."

Nuri gave her shoulders a squeeze. "You'll do great." After a pause, she added. "You miss her, don't you?"

"My mom?"

Nuri nodded. "Your voice hitches ever so slightly whenever you mention her."

No one had said that to her before. No one had ever noticed. Chiara wasn't surprised. Nuri had come to know her better than most of her friends back home. Though they'd only met a few weeks back, when Chiara had just arrived in Bali, Chiara felt closer to her than anyone she could name. Besides Marco. But sibling closeness was an entirely different matter. In Nuri, she'd found the closest thing to a sister she'd ever had.

"I talk to her all the time," she admitted. "In my head. I swear I can hear her respond. Her sweet gentle voice, reassuring me, encouraging me."

Nuri gave her shoulders another affectionate squeeze in silence.

Chiara fought back a tear and sniffled on a small laugh. "I'm not quite sure what she'd say about what I'm about to do here tonight, though. I'm guessing she'd tell me to go for it. As she often did when she was still here."

Nuri chuckled. "She'd also say you were brave and smart and clever. Because all those things are true."

"Thanks, Nuri. Helps to hear that."

The other woman glanced at the smart watch on her wrist. "You are also not great with time. You're running late again."

"Oh, no!"

Nuri gave her a gentle nudge. "If you hurry and the elevator cooperates, you'll make it to his penthouse in the nick of time."

Five minutes later, Chiara released a sigh of relief that her friend had been right. Right on the dot, she was punching in the code Evan had given her that would grant her entrance to his penthouse suite. The rush of adrenaline to make it here on time did nothing to soothe her frazzled nerves, however.

What if she made a fool of herself? Or used the wrong word? Worse, what if she made a terrible faux pas and inadvertently insulted one of the gentlemen? She was debating whether to turn around and send Evan her regrets when he rounded the corner of the hallway. He appeared to be adjusting his cufflinks. He stopped in his tracks when he saw her. His eyes grew wide.

Chiara tried to stamp down on her panic. Why did he look surprised? She was here at the time he'd told her. And why did this man make her so nervous and unsettled? He'd been nothing but friendly and congenial with her since they'd met. A complete gentleman in every way.

A small voice in her head answered her question. *Because you see him as an attractive virile man and not a gentle man at all.*

She cleared her throat. "Sorry, I should have announced myself. But I just arrived seconds ago."

He blinked at her. "No. Don't apologize. It's just…you look…spectacular."

Oh, no! She'd overdressed. This was supposed to be a business dinner meeting, after all. But he wasn't exactly clad in casual attire, either. The dark navy suit he had on had to have been tailored for him. A crisp white shirt and burgundy tie completed an outfit that screamed wealthy, sophisticated, successful businessman. To describe him as handsome would be too simplistic. Plus, he had the most kissable lips. The man probably had women trailing him everywhere he went.

Still. He appeared rather stunned the way he was looking at her. "If there's enough time, I can go change," she stammered out the words. Already she'd made a big mistake, it appeared.

Evan's reply was quick, almost brisk. "Don't you dare."

Okay. Chiara motioned to her midsection. "So, this is okay, then?"

He nodded once. "More than okay. Way to impress them immediately upon entry."

Her shoulders sagged with relief. Phew. "Oh. Thank you. It's just, the way you were looking at me, I couldn't be sure if I'd met the dress code."

He smiled at her. "My apologies. I didn't mean to alarm you. Trust me. What you have on is perfect."

Thank heavens for that. Chiara had no idea what she might have replaced the dress with if he'd asked her to change. It wasn't as if she had a full wardrobe. Traveling the world backpacking and working odd jobs didn't exactly accommodate for the latest fashions.

Which reminded her just how utterly out of place she was going to feel at a business dinner. Too late now, though.

Evan held his arm out to her. "Shall we?"

As she went to place her hand in the crook of his elbow, he appeared to give her another once-over. Something flickered behind his eyes. Huh. If she didn't know better, she might think he was showing genuine male interest.

Right. She had to push that thought aside this very minute. Men like Evan Kim didn't often fall for hotel housemaids. She would do well not to forget that over the course of tonight.

Within minutes, they were walking into the main dining room of the hotel. Chiara felt a strange sensation of altered reality, like none of this was real. As if she were an actress in a movie or a play. She'd never entered this room without a cleaning cart. Now, she was about to dine here, sitting at a table with international titans of the tech industry. As the guest of one of those titans who also happened to be one of the most handsome men she'd ever laid eyes on.

Don't go there, Chiara.

Was that her voice in her head or her mom's? Either way, it was sound advice.

Evan must have sensed her discomfort. "You all right?" he asked, giving her arm an ever so slight squeeze.

She nodded. "Yes. I guess. Just feel a little out of place. Even though I've been in this room countless times." *To clean it*, she added silently to herself.

"Believe it or not, so do I."

"I don't. Believe it, that is."

His response was a soft chuckle.

"Well, for someone who doesn't think she fits in, you sure seem to be turning a lot of heads."

She didn't really believe that, either. If anything, Evan was the one most likely garnering all the attention. Especially among the females in attendance. More than a few were outright staring in their direction. Their attention most definitely didn't seem focused on her.

Evan glanced around the room. "I don't see them. They must be running late." He led her toward the bar. "How about a drink while we wait?"

She immediately shook her head. "I shouldn't. Not if I want to keep my wits about me."

He lifted an eyebrow. "You sure? It might help to calm your nerves a bit. Though I want to assure you, you have no reason to be nervous whatsoever." He leaned over onto the bar. "I'm the one who should be apprehensive here."

Chiara studied his chiseled profile. Steely determination was clear in his expression. Evan Kim was not a man accustomed to losing out on what he pursued.

"This deal means a lot to you."

He motioned for the bartender. "It does, indeed."

"Why exactly? If you don't mind my asking."

He shrugged. "AI is where the industry is headed. I want to be in front of the game."

That was no doubt his surface reason. Something told her his personal reasons ran much deeper. She found herself very curious about what they might be. Maybe she'd even get a chance to ask him sometime tonight.

Then again, why would he bother to tell her anything personal about himself? She was merely here to help him with a business meeting. Technically, she was his employee. Strictly professional. By this time tomorrow, they'd both be on their separate ways with Evan hopefully richer with a business deal and her richer with some much-needed extra cash. She might not ever lay eyes on him again.

She had no business feeling the sense of sadness that washed over her at that thought. "On second thought, I think I will have a glass of wine, after all," she told him when the bartender arrived.

"You got it."

He ordered a straight bourbon for himself and something that sounded very French for her. When their glasses arrived, Evan scanned the dining area once more. His eyes landed on a pair of gentlemen just entering through the doorway. "There they are."

Chiara followed his gaze to where two middle-aged gentlemen in expensive-looking suits stood, scanning the restaurant.

"Showtime," Evan said in her ear. He took her free hand in his and led her toward the two men. The warmth of his palm against her skin sent tingles down her spine. Wow. She really had to get a grip here. In her defense, she hadn't felt a man's touch in close to two years now. That had to be why she was reacting this way to one she'd barely just met.

She didn't have time to reflect on that thought much longer as they approached the two gentlemen.

"*Buonasera*," she offered when they reached their side. In somewhat broken Italian, she explained who she was and why she was there.

By the time they were seated at their table, Chiara felt relaxed enough that her pulse had slowed somewhat. The businessmen were very friendly and full of laughter. And her Italian seemed to be passable enough to move the conversation forward. When things got technical, Evan was able to take over with the necessary terms.

But then one of the men asked her a question. For the life of her she couldn't understand what he'd said. She stared at him blankly for several seconds. A cold wave of panic washed over her as she scrambled to decipher what he'd been asking. Suddenly, she felt Evan's warm hand on her knee under the table. He gave her a small squeeze of encouragement. Darned if it didn't work. Chiara mentally worked through the words she recognized and filled in the rest. The man had been asking about Evan's supply chain contacts.

She interpreted the question to Evan who told her what to say in response.

Crisis averted, the conversation resumed smoothly once more. All in all, she would have called the evening a success. By the look on his face, Evan seemed to be thinking along the same lines. Chiara had to acknowledge the sense of pride coursing through her at the moment. She'd done it!

Thanks for the early language lessons, Mama.

If only she could have told her mother how she'd been able to put it to use.

CHAPTER THREE

EVAN HAD TO resist the urge to grab Chiara about the waist and spin her around in circles. It was hard to keep a lid on his glee.

"Well, what did you think?" she asked. "How'd it go?"

"I think you've earned every penny of your fee. In fact, I think your performance deserves a bonus on top of what we agreed to."

She smiled widely even as she lifted her hands in protest. "I can't accept any kind of bonus. You're already paying me too much as it is."

She was right, of course. He'd doubled the amount he was to have paid the original translator, even when taking into account travel and lodging expenses. Chiara didn't need to know that, however.

"Nonsense. I'll wire the funds into your account as soon as we get back to the suite."

She cleared her throat. "We?"

Maybe he was being presumptuous, but he couldn't seem to help himself. "I have a bottle of fine Cristal chilling up there in an ice bucket. And I'm inviting you to come celebrate with me."

"You were expecting things to go well, then? A true optimist."

Ha! He chuckled out loud at that. If she only knew how wrong she was. "Let's just say I had a lot of faith in my newly found Italian-American assistant."

She bit her lip, a look of concern washing over her features. "Um… Not to be a killjoy or anything…"

He knew what she was getting at. "You're thinking how nothing has actually been confirmed."

She nodded once. "That's exactly what I was thinking. I didn't hear anything, in Italian or English, that sounded like any kind of confirmation, Evan. No one mentioned signing on the dotted line just yet. Only that you could expect to hear from them."

He had to agree. She was absolutely right. Still, the evening had gone off swimmingly. And he'd take victories when he could. Even the small ones.

He held his hand out to her. "There's still reason to celebrate, though, isn't there? They were clearly impressed by you, and I didn't hear them say no."

She bit her lip again. Despite seeming a bit on the spontaneous side, Chiara Pearson was also clearly a worrier. "I suppose…"

"Come on." He gently took her by the elbow and began to guide her out of the room. "Help me enjoy that champagne. We'll worry about the next step when we hear back."

Evan found he'd timed it all well when they got back to the penthouse. The champagne was perfectly chilled. He uncorked the bottle and poured some into one of the flutes on the food service cart, then handed it to Chiara before pouring for himself. "To you and your language skills, Ms. Pearson."

She performed a small bow before taking a sip. Her eyes grew wide as she swallowed. "Wow, this is delicious. And I thought I might be too full after that dinner."

"I find there's always room for good champagne. Though one should sip slowly," he added with a chuckle after she'd taken something of a gulp.

Several minutes of comfortable silence passed before she spoke. "I've never been up here before. Not even to clean."

"Oh?"

She shook her head, studied the room. "They give the penthouse to the more experienced housekeeping staff." After a pause, she added, "I'm still considered a newbie here. Even though I grew up in the hotel business."

"You did?"

She nodded. "My family owns the Grand York Hotel in Manhattan."

He'd certainly heard of it. If he was recalling correctly, The Grand York was known for classic luxury.

She walked over to the glass wall overlooking the beach and sea beyond it. "What a breathtaking view."

He had to admit he hadn't really noticed. Now, as if seeing it through her eyes, he saw what she meant. The scene before them was rather extraordinary. Water huts dotted the crystal blue water. Silvery moonlight bathed the sand and ocean, glittering upon every surface.

"Good thing they don't send me up here to clean," Chiara said.

"Why is that?"

"I could spend hours up here just staring outside."

Before he could answer, his phone vibrated in his pocket. A call from overseas he had to take. "Excuse me for a moment, please."

When he returned a few minutes later, Chiara was seated on the couch, slumped in her spot, her head resting back against the cushion behind her. Her eyes weren't completely closed but close enough to it.

He cleared his throat softly so as not to startle her. Despite his attempt, she jolted upright at the sound.

"I'm so sorry," she said, straightening and glancing around her as if disoriented and not sure where she was. "I'm just so tired."

He surprised himself with his next words. "Then stay."

She gasped and turned to look at him.

"Just relax for a bit tonight," he quickly added. "You've earned yourself some downtime, I'd say. If my calculations are correct, you've been working in some way or another for about eighteen hours."

She gave a brisk shake of her head and stood up rather slowly. "I'm afraid I can't. It's late enough as it is." She didn't meet his eyes, her gaze focused wholly on her feet.

Great. He'd rattled her with his clumsy invitation. Setting his own flute down, he stepped closer to her. He could smell the fruity scent of her shampoo, the sweet bubbly on her breath. "Chiara, it is indeed late. There's plenty of room here. The sofa is a pullout and it appears quite comfortable. There's no need to venture out at this hour. Just spend the night."

This time her gasp was downright loud.

He gave her a reassuring smile. "You can stay in the main bedroom. It locks from the inside," he told her. "You won't even have to see me until the morning."

"I'd hate to make you sleep on a pullout bed."

"After what you accomplished for me at dinner, it's the least I can do. And trust me, I've slept in worse."

She looked skeptical but she wasn't saying no. She glanced over her shoulder in the direction of the master room. "The bed is large and soft," he nudged.

"It's not so much the bed."

"Then what?"

She closed her eyes and released a sigh. "It's just— It's been so long since I've been in any kind of private shower stall. The hostel I'm staying at has three shared ones. There's always a wait. And the water is always cold."

Evan could hear clear longing in her voice. About a shower. Sometimes he took the privileges in his life for granted. Chiara reminded him just how much. "I see." He leaned over closer and winked at her. "The shower head has five different settings. Oh, and there's also a full-size Jacuzzi tub in there."

Her mouth formed a small *o*. "That is tempting, I must admit."

Tempting was an adequate word. For his mind had just traveled to all sorts of forbidden places when he'd mentioned the Jacuzzi. He pictured Chiara submerged in the water surrounded by thick white bubbles. Naked, in the very next room.

He gave a slight shake of his head to clear it. The woman just wanted to bathe. "That settles it, then."

"I don't know, Evan."

He took her by the shoulders, gave them a slight squeeze. "Stay. Take a shower. Or a bath. Do both."

She laughed in response.

"You'd be doing me a favor," he told her. "Again."

She lifted an eyebrow. "How so?"

"Simple. If you insist on leaving, I'll have no choice but to walk you to your place. Then I'll have to walk all the way back."

"I wouldn't make you walk me."

"What kind of gentleman would I be if I didn't insist on doing so?"

She glanced toward the master once more. Finally, with a resigned sigh, she nodded in agreement. "Sure. I'll stay, then. Thank you."

The pleasure that rushed through him at her

acceptance was immediate and rather surprising. It made no sense. He had to chalk it up to appreciating the good fortune of finding someone like her when he needed it most. Someone who spoke Italian and needed extra money so she could travel for the holidays. He'd almost forgotten how much importance others gave to the Christmas season. All the traditions, the celebrations. None of it mattered to him. Christmas was just another day. One he'd spent mostly alone in his room while growing up, on the latest computer his parents had gifted him. His mom and dad were never around during the holidays, preferring to travel to exotic locations rather than spend it at home with their only child.

"I have a large T-shirt you can sleep in and some sports shorts with a drawstring waist," he offered, turning back to the topic at hand.

His offer was simply the act of a savvy businessman, Evan tried to tell himself. It might even be considered a bonus for the fine work she'd done for him tonight. Or what if the Italians had further questions and he needed her to translate once more? Evan needed her to be rested and ready in that case. And that was all he needed from her.

He sighed as those thoughts were immediately shut down by a critical voice in his head.

He was making excuses. Truth be told, Evan wasn't sure why he wanted her to stay so badly. He only knew he wasn't quite ready to say goodbye to her just yet.

She slept like a baby. Chiara couldn't even remember the last time she'd slumbered so soundly. Definitely not since she'd left home. Maybe even before that. And she had Evan to thank for it.

With a yawn and a stretch, she slowly made herself get out of bed. The shirt he'd given her was several sizes too big and hung on her curves like a sack. She hadn't bothered with the shorts. Aside from a restful night of sleep, she felt clean and refreshed. In fact, it was a wonder her skin wasn't pruned and wrinkly all over. After spending a good amount of time in the Jacuzzi, she'd then taken a long hot shower. She didn't regret it the slightest bit. When was the next time she'd get a chance to enjoy such indulgence?

In fact, she was going to go take another long shower before venturing out of the room and heading back to her regular non-luxurious life.

A wave of sadness washed over her. After today, she'd probably never get a chance to come back into this room. Not even as an employee.

She also wouldn't see Evan again. That, she had to admit to herself, was the real reason for the doldrum. The chances of meeting someone like him ever again were slim to none.

Thinking back to the meeting last night, she recalled how utterly in his element he was. Despite not speaking the language of his potential investors, Evan was fully in control throughout the entire night. He drove the conversation and made sure all his points were clearly communicated. It wasn't hard to see why he was so successful at such a young age. She had no doubt he would not only strive but reach even higher heights.

Charming. Successful. Charismatic. Devilishly handsome—the man looked like something out of a magazine cologne ad for heaven's sake.

Maybe she should run the shower cold. A giggle bubbled up her throat. *As if.* She was going to take the longest shower with the hottest water she could stand while she had the chance.

Half an hour later, she had to accept the reality. It was time to unwrap the thick Turkish towel and put last night's dress back on, then make her exit. She couldn't exactly walk out of here wearing Evan's T-shirt and gym shorts.

And it was time to thank the man who had

made her night of excitement and luxury possible. Then say goodbye to him.

A lump formed at the bottom of her throat, and she had to swallow it down.

Best to just get it over with. It was time to bid the man adieu and get back to her own mundane life. One where she still had to figure out how to earn some more of the cash she needed to travel back home. What Evan paid her last night would help, of course. But she still had a ways to go.

The upside was she'd discovered last night that she had yet another option in terms of earning her way. Maybe she could segue this translation ability into a regular gig of some sort.

She had Evan to thank for that new idea as well. And thank him she would. Right now.

But when she left the master bedroom and ventured out in the main living area, he was nowhere to be found.

Huh. Maybe he'd had an early morning meeting. But he hadn't mentioned it last night.

It felt wrong to leave without saying goodbye. *Right. As if that's why you're hesitant to leave while he's gone. Just admit you want to see him again.*

Oh, dear. She had to face the facts. She'd grown overly fond of the man. In the short period of time since she'd smacked into him with a serving tray, she'd developed unexplainable and inconvenient feelings she had no business entertaining. He'd hired her for a simple purpose, and she'd done the job.

Now it was all over.

The truth of that hit her like a ton of bricks. Especially when she heard the door click open and heard him enter the suite. He'd apparently gone for a run. Dressed in a tight sleeveless shirt and running shorts, his skin glowed with the sheen of sweat. He was breathing heavy, wiping at his forehead with the back of his hand. Something shifted in the vicinity of her heart. If she thought he'd looked handsome in a suit, she didn't have the words for the magnitude of sex appeal he exuded at this moment. It took her breath away, the sheer pleasure that slammed into her when he entered the room and walked toward her.

But then she got a look at his expression. Something was terribly wrong. Evan Kim appeared to be furious.

The run hadn't done much to improve his mood. He could have run for miles, though, and it wouldn't have made a difference.

The meeting last night seemed to have gone so well. But not well enough judging by the email Evan had woken up to.

He walked into the suite absentmindedly pulling his sweaty shirt off to find a startled Chiara gaping at him. He must look a mess. Between the sand chafing his shins and the effects of the punishing run he'd just pushed himself through, it was no wonder Chiara appeared to be keeping her distance.

By contrast, she looked beautiful and refreshed, despite wearing last night's dress.

"Uh, good morning?" she said in a gentle voice, then added, "Or is it?"

"How'd you guess?"

"Well, for one, you're scowling. And for another, most people look much less tense after a run."

Evan rubbed his forehead. He had to tell her what had happened. He had to let her know that despite all her charm and competence with Italian, despite all their efforts last night, they had failed.

She didn't give him chance. "Oh, no," she said, covering her mouth with her hand. Sharp cookie. She'd figured it out without him having to say a word.

"So you guessed, I take it," he added, bundling his shirt and tossing it onto the sofa in frustration.

"The Italians said no."

That wasn't entirely accurate but close enough.

"They said they need more time to decide. They have to think it over some more."

She blinked at him, color creeping into her cheeks and her jaw hardening. If he didn't know any better, he'd say she was as upset as he was.

"Tell me exactly what they said."

He reached for his smart phone in his back pocket and called up the email. "See for yourself."

As he watched her read the screen, the message came back to him and reignited his frustration and disappointment.

Very impressed with all you've accomplished. Need to decide about your professionalism. Looking for maturity and stability in our business partners.

And more along those lines.

Chiara's breath had quickened and her eyes narrowed. She was obviously rereading the email more than once. Finally, she handed back his phone.

"I don't understand. Why are they saying these things about you?"

He sighed with resignation. Now, he would have to explain to this sweet accommodating woman all the ways in which his reputation preceded him. Or maybe he could show her.

Calling up the most intrusive of the websites, he clicked on the appropriate link and handed the device back to her. "Here. See for yourself. This is what they're referring to in that email."

She eyed him up and down before taking back the phone and looking at it. Several seconds of awkward silence went past before she finally gave it back to him.

"Well, you seem to have your share of fun."

He scoffed at that. "Trust me, it's all highly exaggerated. They take a well-timed photo and embellish the circumstances. And their readers eat it up."

She crossed her arms in front of her chest. "So, are you like famous or something?"

Despite his ire, he couldn't help but chuckle at her tone. It held utter horror and maybe even some disdain. "Hardly. Only those in very specific circles will even see these hit pieces. Unfortunately, the investors we met with last night would be included in such a group."

"Huh. So now what?"

"Now I have to regroup and somehow figure out how to change their minds."

Her lips tightened in concentration. "You'll have to start by convincing them you're not some sort of party animal."

Evan sighed. "And I have no idea how to do

that. My professional accomplishments should speak for themselves. In a perfect world, they would."

"But all they see is that you're a jet-setting, high-living bachelor," Chiara supplied.

He grunted in frustration. "Well, it's not like I'll be able to acquire a wife and family overnight. I'm not even in any kind of committed relationship at the moment."

At his words, Chiara did that thing where her gaze fell to the direction of the floor. She was probably wondering why he was keeping her here, getting into all of this. She probably had things to do. She was still in last night's dress for heaven's sake. He had no right to impose on her further. It wasn't as if there was anything she could do about any of this.

As much as he hated to see her leave, there really wasn't any reason for her to stay. And he had to figure out where to go from here.

He rammed his fingers through the hair at his crown. "I'm sorry. You probably want to get going. And I could use a shower." He started making his way toward the master bedroom, picking up his discarded T-shirt along the way. "Feel free to order room service. There's an automated coffee bar in the kitchen area."

He sincerely hoped she would take him up on

the breakfast and coffee offer and maybe still be here when he exited the shower. For some odd reason, he wasn't quite ready to see her go. Again, strictly business he tried to tell himself. If there was any way Chiara could help him talk some sense into the Italians, he might still need her.

In any case, he certainly couldn't ask her to stick around any longer. He'd imposed on her long enough.

Besides, he had work to do. He also had to figure out how to appear less like the high-living bachelor the websites described him as. Not that he had any kind of clue how to go about doing that.

And, like he'd just told Chiara, he wasn't even seeing anyone at the moment. No one even came to mind when he considered dating; he hadn't met anyone who'd interested him romantically for quite some time now. In fact, Chiara was the only female who he'd even come close to spending any amount of time with him alone over the past several months.

It hit him as he turned the water on and waited for it to heat up. *Chiara*. Maybe there was, indeed, a way she might be able to help him out with all this.

Sure, it was a harebrained and far-fetched idea that had just sprung into his head. But it just might work. A way to address all his problems. His reputation as far as potential business partners. Attending the wedding. The unwanted attention from the tabloid sites.

Chiara could be the answer to it all.

CHAPTER FOUR

SHE COULDN'T HAVE heard him correctly. Chiara had just made her way to the coffee machine for a much-needed jolt of caffeine when Evan rushed back out of the bedroom. He was still shirtless by the way. So maybe she hadn't been exactly concentrating fully when he said what he did.

She gave her head a brisk shake to try to clear it. "I'm sorry. I could have sworn you just said something to the affect that you and I should tell people we're engaged."

He nodded once. "Uh-huh. That's pretty much what I said."

A giggle burst out of her, and she put her empty cup down before she could drop it. "Evan. What in the world are you talking about?"

Darned if she knew for sure. She was having trouble concentrating. Would it be too awkward to ask him to put his shirt on? The site of his chiseled muscular chest and tanned sweaty skin wasn't making it any easier to focus here. "Did you hit your head on the side of the tub or something?"

"No. I had what you Americans might call a lightbulb moment."

She didn't even know if he was joking. He seemed lucid enough. "Here." He lifted the coffee cup and stepped to the machine. "I'll make you a cup of coffee and we can talk. You have some time?"

Okay. "I guess so. I'm not scheduled until noon."

"Great. How do like your coffee?"

"Lots of cream. Lots of sugar."

"You got it."

"Thanks. But, Evan, just one thing."

"What's that?"

"Could you maybe get dressed first?" She didn't even care how her request sounded. She really couldn't stare at his bare chest any longer, especially not if he was going to try to explain whatever this lightbulb idea of his was.

He gave her a sheepish grin. "Sure thing. Go have a seat. I'll be right back."

Less than five minutes later, he was back after taking what had to be the fastest shower in the history of running water. And thank the heavens above, he'd put on a fresh shirt and khaki shorts. Now maybe he would stop talking nonsense about the two of them pretending to be engaged. Hard to believe that's what he'd really said. How preposterous.

Only, the look of determination on his face had her second-guessing about him backtracking in any way, preposterous or not. He sat across from her at the coffee table and braced his forearms on his knees. "Just hear me out before you say anything. Deal?"

She nodded but her mouth had gone dry. Evan Kim seemed very determined to convince her of whatever he was about to say. Something told her he didn't hear the word *no* often. Well, he was going to have to learn to accept it coming from her. This was beyond ridiculous.

"You said you needed money to get back home in time for Christmas."

He certainly had that right. "Uh-huh."

"And I need to convince several people that I'm on the path of settling down and giving up the life of a freewheeling bachelor."

Well, that statement certainly begged a question. Who else besides the Italian businessmen did he need to convince? She'd have to hold her tongue, though. She'd just promised to hear him out before saying anything. Easier said than done.

"I think we can help each other out."

"How exactly?"

He leaned closer. His breath felt warm on her cheeks. Freshly scrubbed from his shower, she could smell the minty lemon scent of his aftershave. His jet-black hair glistened with dampness. How would it feel to fun her fingers through it? Then she might lower her hand down his cheek and over that chiseled jawline.

Focus! This was important.

"I know this is going to sound crazy," he said now. "But I think it may just work. To pretend we've gotten engaged."

"You're right."

He blinked. "You really think so?"

"About it sounding crazy."

"Just hear me out. All we have to do is pretend we've fallen for each other. At first sight. And we've decided to get married. We knew right away we were meant to be."

He made it sound like some kind of romance novel. "Come again?"

"We met and it was immediate. Chemistry and all that."

Did he even hear himself? Wow, when she'd thought he was driven and determined before, she hadn't even grasped the full extent of his tenacity. She'd never seen anything like it.

"At first sight?" she repeated, hoping he heard how ridiculous such a notion sounded.

He nodded. "Kismet."

"How might it possibly work?" she asked against her better judgment, more out of curiosity than anything else.

He took both her hands in his—absentmindedly, she was sure, whereas she had to make sure to hide her reaction to his touch. Ignore the fact that her heart rate went up a notch. Or how heat seemed to curl in her belly.

Oh, dear. The way she was starting to feel, it was almost as if Evan's words about love at first sight were in fact reality. For her, anyway.

Or it might be more like lust. The man was stunningly alluring.

"I have three high-profile events coming up. You just accompany me to each event as my significant other. We let the cameras snap away while we pose as the besotted couple on the verge of tying the knot."

"Huh."

"Of course, I'd be compensating you for your time. Handsomely. Which solves your problem of travel expenses to America. While in turn solving mine with my reputation."

But why her? "Why would you ask me to do this? There has to be other women who would make more sense to be your fiancée," she stuttered as she said it. No doubt, Evan had countless women in his contact list who would jump at the chance to accompany him around the world, acting lovesick. In fact, they probably wouldn't even need to act. How many women were pining for him right this minute? Why that thought had her muscles clenching, Chiara didn't want to examine. "There must be someone else," she reiterated, resenting how true that statement had to be. Not that it was any of her business. But Evan probably had countless women on speed dial. Women who were probably savvier, prettier, more accomplished, more successful. A bitter taste burned the back of her throat before she swallowed it down and admonished herself. She had no business feeling any kind of way about Evan's history with the opposite sex. "I'm sure there's someone else you can ask this of."

His lips tightened into a thin line. "No. There is no one. Besides, my previous romantic ties all reinforce the image of me I'm trying to erase. Those ladies are no strangers to the party scene themselves. You're the only one."

Heavens, those last few words sent a rush of heat to her cheeks. She knew he didn't mean it in any significant sense, but to hear him say such a thing had her heart thumping.

But he was right about one thing. The entire plan did, indeed, sound crazy. "You can't be serious. This has to be some kind of joke. You're playing with me."

He shook his head in answer. "No joke. No playing. Dead serious."

How could that be? What he was suggesting sounded downright ludicrous. To pretend they were engaged after falling for each other upon meeting?

Even from a practical standpoint, he had to see how little sense he was making with this suggestion. Even if she decided to humor him for a moment. "All the absurdity aside, what you're describing sounds like some kind of acting gig. I have no thespian experience whatsoever. Aside from playing a dancing girl for a middle school production. How would I possibly pull this off?"

"You don't need experience. Just smile for the cameras and follow my lead during conversations."

He made it sound so simple. But the smallest misstep could mean catastrophic embarrassment. Especially for him. She would feel horrible if she messed up at any point along the way. Still…he definitely had a point about her needing the money. "Tell me more about these events."

Chiara's apprehension grew with each word he uttered as he explained. "You're saying I'd be traveling across the world with you."

His smile faltered. "A wedding in Singapore.

Beijing for an investor meeting. And Switzerland for a final business meeting with the Italian AI executive." He dropped her hands and pulled back a bit. "I've got to say, I thought you'd be more excited about that part. Sightseeing at all those places."

She couldn't deny that it sounded like the opportunity of a lifetime. Those were all spots she had on her bucket list. Particularly Beijing. But the circumstances were just so…unconventional.

Don't turn away from opportunities when they present themselves.

Chiara pushed the thought, sounding in her mother's voice, out of her head. Spontaneity was one thing. Insanity was something else.

And that's what this idea was. Insanity. Wasn't it?

She stood up and walked several steps away toward the glass wall. The close proximity wasn't helping. "I'm sorry, Evan. As exciting as this all sounds—"

He held up his hands and interrupted before she could continue. "Don't answer just yet. I have another forty-eight hours before I depart Bali. Just think about it."

She swallowed. "If you insist. Though I don't think time is going to make a difference."

He shrugged. "Maybe, maybe not. I'm just

asking you to give it a think. And think about all those places you'll get to visit. All the sights you'll see."

Wow, he really was playing hard here. Playing to win. He had to know she might never get a chance to visit all those places on her own.

"Chiara, just a few hours to mull it over. That's all I'm asking."

That sounded reasonable enough. Though she wasn't sure how more time was going to make any of this sound any more feasible. Traveling the world with a man she'd just met. Acting as if they were engaged. Pretending to be in love with him.

She nodded silently in answer. Though she knew she was just delaying the inevitable. Just putting off telling in "no". In no uncertain terms.

There was absolutely no way she could accept his offer. Not for any amount of money.

She had to get it over with. Just tell him her answer already that she would be turning him down. The sooner the better. No reason to drag this out any longer than necessary. Then Evan could move on to plan B.

He'd be able come up with a plan B. Wouldn't he?

He wasn't exactly making it easy, however.

She wasn't surprised, of course. Evan Kim was clearly a man who pursued his goals with determination and grit. Since she'd left his penthouse, he'd texted her no less than half a dozen pictures of the luxurious hotel where the wedding would be held as well as majestic scenes from the Great Wall in China. Surely, breathtaking photos of the Swiss Alps would be following in no time. No sooner had she completed the thought than her phone pinged with an attachment message. She ignored it. Not like he was tempting her with breathtaking photos. She was already tempted. A lack of desire to see those sights firsthand was hardly the problem. How many times had her mother mentioned wanting to see the Great Wall?

Mama had never gotten the chance.

Chiara let the sadness at the memory of her mother wash over her as she let herself into her apartment. She'd learned years ago that there was no use fighting it. But she never let herself wallow for too long. That was a slippery slope that she had to avoid for her sanity.

The drab surroundings of the hostel room posed quite a contrast to the suite she'd just spent the night in. That shower and tub had felt like a piece of heaven.

The hotel in Singapore probably had really

nice tubs. And a Jacuzzi pool just like the one she'd enjoyed last night.

She could find out for herself in a few short days.

Chiara squeezed her eyes shut and fell onto the mattress. Why was she even going down this road mentally? Her mind was already made up. She would find another way to get the money. And Evan would find another way to convince his investors. He was adept and resolute and talented. He would figure this out without her. She had no reason to feel guilty that she was letting him down.

Another ping on her phone made her groan out loud. Fully expecting to open a file to a scene of a snowy mountaintop, she was surprised to find a message from her friend instead.

Early lunch? Just made *bakso*. Come by. Lots to share.

Even as she read the note, her stomach grumbled. She loved Nuri's *bakso*. And she could certainly use the company. Nuri wasn't going to believe any of it when Chiara got around to telling her about last night. Or the bombshell proposal Evan had made to her this morning.

Changing and freshening up with haste, she

replied on her way out the door that Nuri could expect her as soon as she could get there. Within minutes, she was seated at Nuri's round wooden table, the aroma of pungent spices and seasoned meat wafting through the air.

They ate in comfortable silence. The warmth of the dish along with the comfort of Nuri's company finally had the knot in her stomach loosening. Nuri leaned back in her chair and popped a piece of bread in her mouth. After swallowing, she shot Chiara a friendly smile. "So, tell me all about last night. How did you do translating?"

Chiara put down her spoon and inhaled deeply. Where to begin answering her friend's question?

"Translating was the easy part. It's the rest that you're not going to believe."

Nuri's eyebrows lifted with curiosity. "Oh? Do tell."

Releasing her breath, Chiara let loose with a torrent of words she could only hope made some semblance of sense. She began by explaining how well she and Evan had thought the meeting had gone, only to be disappointed by the email that morning. Then she told her about spending the night in Evan's suite locked away in the master bedroom. Her friend's eyes grew wide at that part, but she remained silent, listening intently.

"Wow. That's a lot. Will he contact you again, you think? How did you two say goodbye?"

Chiara bit her bottom lip. "That's just it. We might not have."

Amusement mixed in with mild surprise washed over her friend's face. "You didn't? Please explain."

As she told Nuri about Evan's proposal, Chiara realized exactly how harebrained it all sounded when spoken aloud in her own voice. Nuri's eyebrows had lifted practically to her hairline when she was done.

"I don't know, Nuri. On the surface, the answer seems clear. I can't accept such an offer." She rubbed her forehead, deep in thought. "I mean, I just met the man. He seems to be an upstanding person of character. If not a bit of a partier."

"And?"

"And how would I even begin to explain it to my brother or Papa if they ever got wind of any of this?"

"So, you've made your decision, then?"

Chiara's silence was answer enough for her friend.

"Beneath the surface, you're torn," her friend said. "More than a little, it seems."

Chiara puffed out a frustrated breath. "I guess I am. I can't help but keep remembering all the times my mom told me about wanting to travel to all these places. Particularly the Great Wall in Beijing. And she loved the mountains and snow. I know she would have jumped at the chance to visit the Swiss Alps."

Chiara pulled out her cell phone and called up the photo she looked at daily. A picture of a piece of notebook paper; the original was safely tucked away in a drawer at home in New York. The paper was wrinkled and faded from constant handling. Hence, the need for the snapshot. Not that there really was a need at all. She practically had the words on the screen memorized.

"Is that the list?" Nuri asked, emphasizing the last two words as if she referred to a sacred item. In many ways, it was just that. Sacred.

"Yes. The bucket list my mom helped me write of all the places I wanted to visit and the things I wanted to do as soon as I became an adult."

The memories came rushing back as she recalled the afternoon. Sitting down and writing in a notebook was the last thing she'd wanted to do. She would have rather ran upstairs and cried into her pillow after what had happened earlier that day. But her mother wouldn't hear of it. As usual, she'd been right. "Did I ever tell you how the list came about?" she asked her friend rhetorically, as she already knew the answer. Chiara would have remembered sharing such a memory with her friend.

Nuri leaned closer. "Tell me."

"I'd just gotten rejected by my high school crush. I'd planned an elaborate way to ask him to the main event of high school."

"Oh?"

She nodded. "A prom. I planned it for weeks, the perfect prom-posal."

"Prom-posal?"

"An elaborate way to ask someone to the prom. The last major dance in high school before graduation. A really big deal."

"And you wanted to ask this boy to take you."

"Oh, yes. Not just any boy. The star running back on the football team. Popular and handsome. I didn't really think it through."

"What happened?"

She cringed as she called up the memory. "I dressed up in a fancy gown, did my hair and makeup. And waited outside the locker-room door with a big sign for him to exit with the rest of the football team."

Nuri visibly winced. "Uh-oh. I think I can guess what happened."

"He turned me down flat. In front of all his teammates and buddies. They all started laughing. At me." Chiara actually laughed as she explained. Funny how she could laugh about the incident now. At the time, it had seemed so tragic to her teenage psyche.

"Ouch."

"Yeah, it hurt. Afterward, all I wanted to do was wallow in my room and cry. I told my mom in no uncertain terms that I would never take a chance again. No more risks. It was too painful."

"Your mom had other ideas."

Chiara nodded. "She sure did. She told me I had so many more adventures ahead of me. And that we would sit down and start planning some of them right that very minute." A rock formed at the base of her throat as she spoke, and tears stung her eyes. Her mom had known exactly how to combat her sadness and come up with the perfect way to get her focused on the future instead of one boy's rejection. Hence, the bucket list. It mostly consisted of traveling to several exotic locations.

She'd already checked off Bali. And Mexico, thanks to a class trip senior year. A couple of spots in central Europe when she first started backpacking. But there were so many boxes left. So many more places she wanted to see while she had the chance.

Evan was giving her a once-in-a-lifetime

chance to check off some of those boxes. All expenses paid.

Nuri braced her hand on her chin over the table. "Hmm. What do you think your mom would say to all this? What would she advise you to do?"

Chiara glanced once more at the screenshot on her phone. The answer was all too clear.

CHAPTER FIVE

CHIARA WAS STILL ruminating on that question ninety minutes later as she packed her cleaning cart. In some ways, she felt as if her mother was always with her, guiding her spiritually. But how could Chiara possibly say what Gabriela Pearson may have said about her daughter's current predicament?

She could guess what Papa and Marco would say if they ever got wind of all this. A resounding *no* from both.

As if she'd summoned it, her phone began to vibrate in her pocket, then sounded her brother's ringtone. Darn, she usually texted him before her shift, but she'd been too preoccupied this afternoon. Marco had a tendency to worry. In some ways, it was as if she had two fathers.

She picked up before it could go to voice mail. He was just going to keep calling if he didn't talk to her live. "Hey, sis. Haven't heard from you. How're things down in paradise?"

Paradise wasn't quite what she'd call this supply room with its metal shelves and scrub mops hanging on the walls. "Oh, you know. Living a fantasy."

He chuckled at that. "Just think, you'll be home in a few short weeks to tell us all about it."

Chiara felt the now-familiar tightness in the pit of her stomach every time the subject of traveling back home came up. She did her best to ignore it. "I'll give you all the juicy details as soon as I set eyes on you."

"Waiting with bated breath." Was it her imagination or did Marco sound off? Distracted?

No doubt, it was just the upcoming holidays he had on his mind. She had her own issues.

For a split second, she wanted to just give in to what felt so natural and confide in her big brother. He'd always been there for her while they'd been growing up. Even before Mama was gone. Her current predicament was made all that much harder because she couldn't lean on him emotionally. Because then she'd have to tell him that she spent all the money she'd earned and given away what their father had sent her to cover her travel expenses.

The only thing that might come close to having her father disappointed in her would be for her brother to feel that way. But it pained her on such a deep level. She could really use his feedback right now.

Except maybe there was some small way he could provide it. Between his studies and his hospitality experience, Marco had a lot of contacts. She might be able to pick his brain, after all.

"Hey, I have a question for my big brother," she began.

"Shoot."

"Between the hotel and your school buddies, would you happen to know anything about a young entrepreneur by the name of Evan Kim? I thought maybe you may know who he is."

"Hmm," he answered. "Name's not ringing a bell. Why are you asking about him?"

"There's some sort of tech convention here at the hotel in Bali. He's one of the names being tossed around as an up-and-comer in the field. Has done so much at such a young age…yada yada." Everything she'd just said was the absolute truth.

Her brother chuckled. "We do have one regular guest who's a titan in the industry. I also consider him a friend. I have his contact info. I could drop him an email and see what he knows about the guy."

Knowing more about the man would certainly help. Basic research. She was considering a job offer, after all. Though it was a rather unorthodox one. "Thanks, Marco. I'm just curious. And you know how I can get when I'm curious about something."

He laughed again. "You're the ultimate researcher." She knew the part he wasn't voicing out loud. Neither her brother nor her father could understand why she hadn't put her curiosity and research skills to use by finishing her university studies.

"I'll call you as soon as he gets back to me," Marco said, then bid her goodbye.

As it happened, that didn't take long. Chiara was in between rooms about an hour later when her brother's ringtone sounded again from her pocket.

"That was fast," she answered after clicking on the call.

"My friend replied fast. Caught him waiting on a delayed flight so he had some time. He had a lot to say about the name you gave me."

Chiara's heart fluttered in her chest. No matter what she decided to do about his proposal, she didn't want to hear anything untoward about Evan. Why that was, she wasn't ready to examine just yet. "And? Was it good?"

"All good. Described him as a wunderkind who developed his own app at the ripe old age of nineteen. That's just how he made his first couple million. He's had his hands in various technological ventures ever since."

What about his personal life? Chiara didn't voice the question out loud. "Is that it?"

"For the most part. Lately he's been labeled as something of a partier. But I was told that seems to be a lot of hype. A way to get clicks from a certain crowd who follows this stuff."

Overhyped or not, the rumors were certainly problematic when it came to convincing investors.

"So, to rest your curiosity," her brother continued, "he appears to be a stand-up guy."

Relief washed over her in waves. "Well, it sounds like Evan Kim is on the up and up."

Someone behind her in the hallway loudly cleared their throat. Chiara froze where she stood. The sting of embarrassment burned her cheeks. She didn't have to turn around to know who was right behind her and had just heard every word.

Closing her eyes with a resigned sigh, she turned over her shoulder before opening them again. Yep. She'd been right. Evan.

He leveled a steady gaze on her face. Chiara willed for the ground to open under her feet and dropped her several floors below. Did Bali ever suffer earthquakes? She wouldn't mind a mild one right about now. No such luck.

Evan crossed his arms in front of his chest. "Sounds like you're checking up on me, Ms. Pearson."

Evan stifled a chuckle at the look of utter horror on Chiara's face when she turned to find him standing in the hallway. When he hadn't heard from her, he'd begun to grow restless, even though she had ample time before she owed him an answer. Still, it'd been hard to focus on anything else. He hadn't been looking for her just now per se. He'd describe it more as wandering around in the hope she would show up where he was.

And it had worked.

Though Chiara was looking at him as she if she wished she were anywhere else. He held up both hands, palms up. "Look, I don't blame you for looking into who I am. In fact, you'd be remiss if you didn't."

Her features relaxed as he spoke. "It was the most basic of inquiries."

"Did I pass?"

"A minus, give or take."

He clutched his chest in mock horror. "Less than an A plus. My former tutors would be beside themselves to hear it."

"It can be our secret."

"What about our other prospective secret?"

"You mean the secretly fake engagement?"

He nodded. "You're clearly asking around about me. Does that mean you've given it any more thought?"

She ignored his question, throwing out one of her own. "What are you doing here, anyway? On this floor?"

He pointed a playful finger at her. "You're good at avoiding answering questions."

She tilted her head. "Really? You just did that exact same thing."

Evan pinched the bridge of his nose. They were going around in circles here. "Give me another chance to continue trying to convince you."

She leaned back against the wall, crossed her ankles.

Evan had an urge to brace his hands on either side of her head where she rested against the wall. She had her hair up in some kind of haphazard ponytail that left curly tendrils around her face. Her uniform clung to her in all the right places.

Something had to be wrong with him. There was nothing particularly enticing about a housekeeping uniform. Except the way Chiara wore it.

"I'm listening. What do you have in mind?" she prompted.

He returned to the matter at hand "I'm extending you an invitation. One I hope you'll accept."

She scrunched her nose. "Like a business meeting or something? Listen, Evan, we can go over numbers until sunset. I know you're willing to pay handsomely. Numbers are not the issue."

He shook his head. "That's not it. No business. Just some pleasure."

Just some pleasure.

Chiara's heart thudded in her chest at his words. Made all the worse when he continued, "Can you come by around seven? We can grab a bite to eat and go from there."

She shrugged, feigning an indifference she didn't feel. "Sure. Why not? I have nothing going on tonight." Or any other night in the foreseeable future. Unless, of course, she went globetrotting around the world with Evan.

Dear saints. Was she really thinking about saying yes? When exactly had that tide turned?

"Bring a swimsuit and a change of clothes," Evan said, distracting her.

"A swimsuit?"

He winked at her. "Trust me."

If he only knew, Chiara thought, watching him walk away. It appeared she was beginning to do just that. For she had every intention of heading to his suite at the end of her shift.

Which couldn't come soon enough.

Hours later, by the time she rolled her cart back into the supply room, Chiara was more than ready to find out exactly what Evan had in mind with his latest *invitation*.

Within half an hour of clocking out, she was in the elevator that led to the penthouse suite with her swimsuit and a towel tucked in a tote bag hung over her shoulder. She'd changed into a loose-fitting top that looped into a bow at the side of her waist over a pair of slim-fitting capri pants.

She hadn't thought to ask about any kind of dress code for dinner. What if Evan had something more formal in mind? So she was relieved when the elevator doors opened to find him dressed just as casual in khaki shorts and a form-fitting white T-shirt that accented every inch of his muscled chest and arms. For a successful app-and-code developer, the man certainly must have made time for regular workouts. Or maybe he was just naturally chiseled.

"Right on time," he greeted her with a wide smile. But instead of inviting her in, he stepped into the lift with her and keyed the button for the lobby floor.

"Are we eating on the beach, then?"

He shook his head, watching the elevator panel. "Nope."

"Then where?"

"You'll see." He pointed to her tote bag. "Did you bring a swimsuit?"

"Uh-huh."

"Good. I was thinking we might swim first. Depending on how hungry you are. I'll let you decide."

Where was he taking her? "If we're not eating on the beach, then how would we swim?"

He gave her another wink. "Patience, Ms. Pearson. Like I said, you'll see."

There was a car and driver waiting for them when they left the lobby and stepped outside.

"It's not far," he explained as he helped her in the back seat, then settled in next to her.

Unlike her, the driver must have been told in advance where they were going. He slipped into the chaotic, noisy traffic and moved them along until they reached a Lagoon Villa Chiara knew to be one of the most exclusive tourist attractions in the area.

She was speechless as he escorted her out of the car and along the wooden pathway leading to one of the larger bungalows sitting atop the water.

A private table had been set up for them and

the satay was sizzling on an open flame pit. Platters of vegetable and exotic fruit had already been set out.

"Wow," was all she could come up with to say.

"This is one of my favorite spots in Bali. I come here as often as I can."

She took in the scene before her. The jade color of the water, the tiki torches lit up with flames leading up the wooden pathways. "I don't blame you."

"So, did you want to eat first?" he asked.

Here stomach answered for her with a loud grumble.

Evan threw his head back with a laugh. "Dinner it is."

The satay was some of the best she'd ever tasted. Seasoned skewers of chicken and lamb served on a bed of *nasi goreng*, Indonesia's national dish of specialty fried rice. With a side of crisp grilled vegetables, it all made for a scrumptious meal her taste buds wouldn't soon forget.

"What brought you to Bali, anyway?" Evan suddenly asked between bites of fried rice. "I'm guessing it wasn't to work in a touristy hotel down here?"

She shrugged. "I got bit by the travel bug about a decade ago. Bali was one of the places on the list."

Evan didn't need to know that it was more her mother's list, and her mother's bug for that matter. Chiara had promised Mama just before losing her that she would do all she could to travel to as many of the spots her mother had wanted to see before illness robbed her of the opportunity.

No, she didn't want to get into any of that with Evan right now.

Even a decade later, the wound was too fresh, the loss too deep. She might completely fall apart if she tried to talk about it. The same as always.

He lifted his glass up toward her in salute. "Well, I'm glad you decided to come to Bali. Now."

Come to think of it, so was she. No matter what tomorrow held, this night was sure to become a cherished memory. One for the journals to tell the grandchildren about.

Though she would leave out the part about how attracted she was to her dinner companion. Or how he was trying to convince to fake marry him.

Just when Chiara thought she couldn't take another bite, the server arrived with a tray of cassava cakes. Spongy and syrupy, they made her mouth water despite how full she already felt. "How well do you know this chef?" she asked in a teasing voice even as she reached for one. "I heard cassava can be dangerous, poisonous even, when not cooked properly."

He playfully pulled the dish away before she could reach one of the pieces. "Then I won't have you risk it. I need you too much."

Wow. The man certainly knew what he was doing, didn't he? As if the setting and this romantic dinner wasn't enough to sway her decision, now he was tempting her with his words. Had anyone ever come out and explicitly said they'd *needed* her before? Growing up in the family she had, it was implied as a matter of fact. But when had it ever been acknowledged with words to her directly?

She couldn't recall.

"Here." Evan grabbed a cake off the tray. "I'll go first." He popped the entire morsel in his mouth at once.

"My taste tester?"

He gave her a wide smile and a wink. "We might be on the verge of insulting the chef here," he warned. "Hopefully, he's not listening."

She pulled the tray over to her side of the table. "If he is, our only means of atonement is to finish every last piece."

It didn't take long before nothing but crumbs

remained. Chiara was certain she'd eaten at least two pieces more than Evan had. Oh, well, it wasn't often a girl was treated to a gourmet dinner in a bungalow sitting in a pretty lagoon.

Evan took a sip of his water. "There's a changing area around the back if you want to go put your suit on. If you still want to swim, that is."

She nodded with enthusiasm. "Yes. I can't believe it hasn't rained at all the past few days. You better believe I'm going to take advantage."

He was already in the water when she returned. Not normally shy while wearing a swimsuit, something felt different about this time. Evan tore his gaze away a little too quickly; he appeared to be looking at anything except in her direction. Was he simply being a gentleman until she could get into the water? Or was there another reason he was avoiding looking at her at all costs?

"Are you going to get in or not?" he asked after several beats had passed.

There was something to be said for jumping straight out of a bungalow where you'd just had dinner into a refreshing body of water. Another experience she wouldn't soon forget.

Taking a couple steps back to get a running start, she performed what her brother would have called a bomb cannonball and jumped in.

Sometimes you just have to jump right in and not overthink. Mama hadn't been talking about swimming so much as life in general.

As Chiara submerged completely below the surface, she felt the cooling water soothe her nerves and let it relieve some of the tension and anxiety of the past several days. Ever since she'd given away her travel money.

Chiara envied the fish that could stay down here indefinitely. In an environment so peaceful and serene. The noiselessness beneath was like a balm to her soul. Her mind hadn't been silent in so long. It was so very silent down here under the water. Silent enough that answers became clearer. All the background noise and warnings had faded.

She had her answer. She was going to jump right in, as she had just now into the water. Calmness settled over her. She'd been offered a solution—why in the world would she turn it down?

She held her breath for as long as she could, relishing in the newfound relief that came with her decision. Finally, her lungs began to scream out in complaint. She thrust herself upward with a sputter.

"You were under a long time," Evan said when she resurfaced. "I was about to come down there to see if you needed rescuing."

Maybe she did. As strong and independent as she'd always prided herself on being, maybe at this point in her life, being rescued was exactly what she needed.

CHAPTER SIX

One week later

HE OFFICIALLY HAD a fiancée.

How exactly was an engaged man supposed to behave, anyway? How did a man carry off the experience of being happily committed to someone?

Darned if he knew, Evan thought as he tipped the bellman who had escorted them to their suite, then closed the door behind the young man.

Louis certainly seemed to have gotten the hang of fiancé-ing. The man had been wearing a smile and look of utter contentment since he'd met his bride-to-be. Maybe he could ask him for some pointers. Of course, Evan's particular disadvantage here was that his engagement was a farce. No proposal. No wedding at the end. Just a means to serve a purpose.

No matter. He just needed it to appear real. Just for a few short weeks.

Chiara definitely looked the part. And she would even more so by tomorrow after a visit from a personal shopper in about an hour.

"This view is breathtaking," she said now, staring at the skyline outside the glass balcony doors.

If he were her real intended, he would acknowledge her comment by walking up behind her, wrapping his arms around her waist and pulling her tight against him, back to chest, as they admired the view together.

"I'm glad you like it," he said instead. "We'll be staying here until the wedding."

He saw her visibly tense at the last word. The urge to go to her grew exponentially, simply in comfort. "No need to be nervous, Chiara. Everyone will love you."

That might have been a bit of a fib. He didn't even know what pleased his parents anymore. Or if they would even make the effort to meet her. Telling Chiara any of that wasn't going to help her nerves, however. He'd somehow managed to dodge her questions about his family during the plane ride by focusing on the code on his laptop while she read a newsmagazine. But he could only dodge for so long.

"I'm just a little anxious about meeting your friends and family, that's all." She bit her bottom lip. "It's so much more nerve-racking than translating for a meeting."

"You'll be fine. Have faith in yourself."

She sighed. "I'll try. Could we maybe go over some details about your family and your friends? Maybe over dinner?"

Evan fought not to visibly shudder at the idea. "I'm afraid I have some things to do tonight. Some deliverables for an international investor."

Her shoulders drooped. "I see."

"Take a look at the room service menu. The hotel restaurant employs a world-renowned chef. Or you can order in from one of the five-star restaurants in the area."

"It's too bad you'll be busy. I was hoping to see a bit of the city the first night."

Before he had a chance to respond to that, the door sounded with the buzz of an arrival.

"Excuse me," Evan said. "That would be the shopper."

The same bellhop was back with the woman and together they hauled in several cases and two full racks of garments.

"What is all this?" Chiara asked, walking over to the racks and fingering a blue silk top.

Was he imagining it or did she sound irked?

She dropped the fabric and turned to him. "I thought I was just being fitted for a dress for the wedding."

Yep. She was definitely annoyed. For the life of him, he couldn't figure out why.

"That's the primary intent," he told her. "But you need other things as well for the next several weeks."

"I had no idea I would be having a full wardrobe fitting. You never mentioned it."

He shrugged. "I said a personal shopper would stop by because you needed a dress for the ceremony, because that was the most important item."

The shopper stood glancing at one of them, then the other, tension clear in her expression. After several seconds of silence, she excused herself and hastily made her way in the direction of the hallway.

"Chiara," he began as soon as he heard the hallway bathroom door shut. "This is only to get you some garments so that you look the part."

Something shifted behind her eyes and her lips tightened into a slim line.

"But I can't afford this, Evan. Any of it. And I certainly don't expect you to purchase me a whole new wardrobe."

What was she talking about? He didn't understand the issue. She seemed to be making one out of nothing. "How is this any different than how the Bali hotel provided you with a housekeeping uniform?" he asked.

She lifted a red silky scarf and held it out to him. "This is very different than a cheap maid's uniform."

"Only in that it's more expensive."

Her eyes grew wide with astonishment at his words. "How do you not hear how that sounds?"

Evan pinched the bridge of his nose and summoned up all his patience. Being in Singapore for Louis's nuptials had him on edge as it was. Everyone from his past life was going to be at this wedding. People he hadn't seen or spoken to in years, including his mother and father.

Perhaps that's why he wasn't handling this well and addressing her objections about the clothing. But it was just clothing, for heaven's sake.

"Look, if it makes you feel better, don't keep the clothes." Though he had no idea what he would do with them. Maybe his assistant would be more enthused about a new wardrobe than Chiara seemed to be. As she looked to be the opposite of enthused. In fact, she appeared downright insulted.

"I just need you to wear them for the duration of this bargain between us. So you can—"

"Right." She held a hand up before he could continue. "So I can look the part. I get it."

Then she turned her back to him to stare out the window once more.

* * *

What had she done?

This whole thing had been a mistake. She'd fallen for Evan's charm and the lure of easy money and committed herself to a deal she now had no way out of.

Now that she was on board, it was clear that she was nothing but a business partner to Evan. He'd been cold and aloof with her on his private jet.

And the clothes! How humiliating. He hadn't even seen much of her wardrobe but had already decided it wouldn't be suitable for the likes of his friends and kin.

Chiara was nothing but a Pygmalion project to help him achieve his latest goal.

Well, she had no one but herself to blame. She should have never expected anything more. It was only three weeks. Then she'd be on her way to see her own family and spend Christmas with those she loved most.

Evan Kim would be a distant memory in no time once she made it back home. A tiny voice in her head mocked that thought and she felt a tug in the vicinity of her chest.

"I'd ask that the items be donated to charity once we are done."

He nodded once. "Of course. That can certainly be arranged."

"Maybe an international women's charity. Or an auction where the proceeds will be used for such a cause."

"Of course. I'll send my assistant a note right away to find a suitable recipient."

With perfect timing, the personal shopper re-appeared in the doorway.

"Let's begin then, shall we?" Chiara asked her with the widest, fakest smile she could muster.

The woman's shoulders sagged in relief, which made Chiara feel a tug of guilt that she and Evan had made her uncomfortable. She strode over to her with her hand extended. "I'm Chiara. Thank you so much for coming today."

She returned the smile and took her hand. "I'm Trina."

"I'll leave you ladies to it, then," Evan said, Chiara couldn't quite bring herself to look at him. "I'll just be in the study, if you need anything."

"Thank you, Evan," she said, keeping her gaze focused squarely on Trina's expression of relief.

He walked away silently.

Chiara walked over to the rack with the more casual outfits. "Where do we begin?"

"Anywhere you'd like." She clenched her hands together. "If you're sure you'd still like to. I can always come back another time." Everything in her voice told Chiara she'd much rather not do that.

"Absolutely not. I just wasn't aware of exactly what Evan had in mind. Just a bit of a shock to see so many items, that's all."

Trina barked out a laugh. "I totally understand. Boyfriends can be so clueless."

"Oh, he's not my boyfriend," Chiara quickly corrected, then remembered why she was here. She and Evan were, indeed, supposed to be romantically involved. That was the whole point, wasn't it?

"Oh?" Trina appeared confused.

"He's actually my fiancé." Close one. Though she wasn't even sure if they were supposed to be announcing it just yet. It wasn't like Evan had given her any kind of guidance. In fact, he'd been downright stone-faced since she'd signed on the dotted line of his contract.

Trina clasped her hands together. "Congratulations!" Her eyes fell to her left hand. Drat. They hadn't even talked about a ring. She might have to say something to him about it.

She cringed when she thought about how uncomfortable that conversation was sure to be. Never in a million years would she have thought she'd be put in the awkward spot of asking after her own engagement ring. A ring that would be the gesture of a complete farce.

"Have you two been together long, then?"

Stick to the story. "No, actually. We just met. You know what they say, about instant attraction and love at first sight."

Trina's smile widened. "Oh! How romantic. Getting engaged so soon after meeting."

Chiara shrugged. "Thanks. Some might call it impulsive. My father always said I'm too spontaneous at times." That was the absolute truth. Though she shuddered to think what her father would say if he saw her now.

She looked up to find Trina watching her with a curious look. Chiara clapped her hands in front of her chest, feigning the excitement of a bride-to-be about to attend her first few events with her intended. "Right. Let's go ahead and get started, then."

For the next hour and a half, Chiara played dress-up. She probably shouldn't admit it to Evan but trying on fancy clothes was more fun than she would have realized. Despite knowing that she wouldn't actually come to own any of it for herself. She pretended she was a fashion model about to walk the runway or sit for a glamorous magazine shoot.

After showing her casual outfits to wear during the day, Trina pulled the rack of dresses over. How in the world would she be able to pick just one? They were all lovely pieces of art that had to be one of a kind.

Finally, she settled on a sapphire-blue silky number that Trina said brought out the hue of her eyes.

They made small talk while Chiara tried on clothing, walking back and forth to the restroom with each new outfit. She didn't think Evan would come back out to the sitting area anytime soon. But Chiara wasn't going to risk being mistaken on that front and have him catch her in a state of mid-dress.

"So, is this your first time in Singapore?" Trina asked. Her delightful accent sounded like poetry to Chiara's ears.

"Yes, I'm looking forward to seeing the city." *When we finally get around to it*, she added silently. Or *if*.

"There's a new place in town. Really good sushi and wontons." She supplied the name of the restaurant and emphasized that Chiara and Evan just had to try it.

"I'll be sure to let my fiancé know." She wasn't going to get used to saying that word anytime soon. If ever.

The other woman surprised her by giving her a mischievous wink and taking her by the hand. "I also want to show you these. They might come in handy for a newly engaged woman."

She lifted the top of a wooden chest to reveal a stash of lingerie folded neatly in a stack, then held up a pantie and bra set made of nothing but lace. Chiara tried to hide her gasp of surprise. She definitely wouldn't be needing those over the next few weeks. But she couldn't help several unwanted images playing in her head. A masculine hand lowering the thin strap off her shoulder, heavy-lidded eyes taking in the picture of her wearing such a thing, his breath warm on her cheek.

Heaven help her, the man in all those images was Evan Kim.

Oh, dear. She had it bad. For a man who wasn't even taking the time to eat dinner with her their first night in one of the most exciting cities on the planet.

Just to get it over with, without having to divulge too much to Trina, she lifted a slip of a negligee and studied it. "I'll take this one."

"That's all?" Trina asked.

She could only nod.

Trina giggled. "Silly me. Of course, a woman like you must have made sure to pack plenty of things like these."

Chiara swallowed her gulp of laughter. If Trina only knew. Her delicates consisted mostly of sports bras and boy shorts made for comfort and nothing else.

Finally, after she'd made her final decisions on which were the most flattering pieces, Trina bid her goodbye. Chiara guessed Evan must have worked out a payment process with her in advance.

The same way he'd done with Chiara for that matter.

Well, she had no right to feel any kind of way about that dismal thought. After all, she was merely an employee fulfilling a contract, too.

After seeing Trina to the door, Chiara couldn't help but pick up the negligee and hold it up to admire its delicate beauty. Too bad no one would ever see her in it save for herself. It felt soft as tissue in her hand. Luxurious and featherlight. She held it up to her body, imagining what it would feel like to wear as she snuggled under the covers in the middle of the night. A sigh escaped her lips at the image.

Evan picked that moment to stride into the room.

Evan was totally unprepared for the sight that greeted him when he walked into the sitting area to find Chiara holding what could only be described as temptation incarnate. He couldn't make himself look away.

He knew he should have stayed in his study. She quickly dropped the item onto the couch behind her, but it was too late. His mind had already processed what it was taking in and proceeded to all sorts of thoughts he had no business thinking.

Like how Chiara would look actually wearing the thing. And how it would feel to take it off her.

Steady there, fella. She's just here on an assignment you hired her for.

Right. He was essentially her boss. He tried to come up with something to say but his mouth had gone dry. Finally, he managed a dry, "Hello."

That's it. Dazzle her with witty conversation to get past the highly awkward moment.

Chiara gave him a smile that was much too tight to be real. "Um…hi. Trina just left."

"Trina?"

"The shopper."

Right. He'd forgotten the woman's name. Heck, he'd come darn close to forgetting his own name. The blasted images still hadn't left his mind's eye.

Evan cleared his throat. "Um, I should have explained exactly why she was here. I didn't mean to throw you a curveball about the clothing."

"It's okay. I overreacted. But I'll still feel better if the clothes are donated…when we're done."

"Of course. As you wish." More awkward silence ensued after that rather useless exchange. What was wrong with him? He'd been with plenty of women, and he'd seen his fair share of racy nightwear. She hadn't even had it on, for heaven's sake. The sight of it really shouldn't have conjured up the wanton images and turned his brain to mush the way it had.

"Trina was lovely," Chiara supplied, clearly looking for ways to keep the conversation going.

"My assistant found her. Through a friend."

"She mentioned a new restaurant nearby. I know you said the hotel chef is world-renowned, but I thought we might try her suggestion instead tonight."

"Whatever you want."

"Great. Thanks."

"You're welcome." For the life of him, he couldn't come up with anything else to say. How lame.

"Well, I should let you get back to work." She pulled her cell phone from her pocket. "I'll see if I can locate the place Trina suggested and see if they'll deliver."

Suddenly, it occurred to him that work was the last thing he wanted to do at the moment. He wanted to enjoy the city, in the company of the woman who had dropped everything to travel the world with him. He'd been so selfish to ask her to stay in their first night. She was probably dying to get out there and take it all in. And he had come close to denying her the chance to do so.

You're selfish, Evan. You only ever think of yourself.

Evan forced the unwanted memory away and made himself focus on the present.

Though, in a way, he supposed he was still being somewhat selfish. For what he said next was just as much for his own sake as for Chiara's.

"You know what? I think we should go out and have that meal at the restaurant."

Her eyes lit up. "You do?"

"Yes. We'll even make a couple stops along the way."

"Oh, Evan, I would love that." Her brows furrowed. "But I thought you had things to do."

He shrugged. "I've just decided it can wait."

Months from now, when Chiara was out of his life, he didn't want to regret any of the decisions he'd made when it came to her.

The work would still be there, more of it in fact. But Chiara would not.

So, for tonight at least, everything else could wait.

And his decision had nothing whatsoever to do with Chiara's new nightwear.

CHAPTER SEVEN

CHIARA COULDN'T GUESS what might have made Evan change his mind. She was just so very happy that he had. She'd been itching to explore the city, probably would have ventured out on her own at some point. She'd been backpacking across several countries for the past two years. Sightseeing alone wouldn't be a new experience for her.

But it was so much more enjoyable with company. Evan's company in particular.

Apparently, she wasn't hiding her excitement very well.

"You look downright giddy, Ms. Pearson," Evan chuckled as they walked out of the hotel lobby and onto the sidewalk.

"Guess it's pretty obvious."

"Are you up to walking?" he asked as they stepped into the cool evening air. "The weather seems mild enough."

She nodded with all the enthusiasm she felt.

"I'd love to. I want to see as much of the city as I can."

Chiara knew she sounded like a little girl on her first trip to Disneyland. But she didn't care. It was exactly how she felt. Singapore was alive around them. Towers that seemed to reach higher than the sky were lit up like neon monoliths. The water of the marina in the distance glistened like liquid diamonds.

Christmas decorations and lights adorned the street. As if Santa's wonderland had moved to a warmer, much more exotic locale. The sights took her breath away.

Within minutes, they had reached the restaurant and were seated at a booth.

The dining area looked like a cross between an old-fashioned American diner and a Michelin-starred restaurant. Chiara gasped as covered bowls of food sped past her ear on some kind of conveyor belt.

Evan chuckled at her reaction just as another bowl flew by.

"I take it you haven't had *kaitenzushi* before."

"Does that mean flying sushi? If so, then yes, you would be correct. I've never had the pleasure."

He laughed at that. "The best translation would be conveyor belt sushi. Various pieces go by—you can pick one you want or special order using the screen." He pointed to a mounted tablet above their table. It was playing some kind of anime cartoon on the screen.

"Here, let's try this one." He opened the bowl that happened to be passing. Two pieces of rolled sushi sat on the plate and they each took one. Chiara popped it in her mouth and began to chew. A burst of flavor exploded over her tongue—delicate fish, a tangy sauce and another subtle taste she couldn't quite place.

"Oh, wow. This is delicious." She took out the next plate without bothering to ask. This dish was just as tasty as the last one. When they were done with the latest rolls, Evan grabbed the two empty plates and slipped them into an open slot at the side of the table.

"How often have you had *kayta*…?" She gave up. There was no use trying to pronounce what he'd called it. "How often have you had conveyor belt sushi?" she asked. She wouldn't have even thought to push the empty plates through the slot, had barely even noticed it was there.

"In Tokyo a few times. The concept originated in Japan. One restaurant on Shibuya Street has three floors with different kitchens and belt systems."

Tokyo. It was one of the cities her mom had talked about visiting. Then again, there weren't that many capitals her mom hadn't been interested in. "I'd like to get to Tokyo someday," she admitted.

He reached across the table to take her hand in his. The warmth of his touch spread from her fingers, through her core and down to her toes. "I have no doubt you'll get to Tokyo, Chiara. You'll love it."

Just as Mama would have.

"My mom and I talked about going there together someday. Before she got sick." Her words came as a shock to her own ears. She hardly ever talked about her mom. Not even to her closest friends. And most definitely not with her brother and father. Speaking about their loss only served to amplify the pain for all three of them. "I really miss her," she found herself confiding.

"When did you lose her?" Evan asked in a gentle voice. He gave her hand a reassuring squeeze.

"About ten years ago." The burn of tears stung behind her eyes, and she swiped them with her free hand before they could fall.

"You were barely more than a teenager."

She nodded, gulping against the lump that had formed at the base of her throat. "It still feels like it happened just yesterday."

"I'm really sorry. I know there are no words that can adequately address the pain of that kind of loss."

"You must feel so happy that you're going to get to see both your parents in a couple of days at your friend's wedding."

Something shifted behind his eyes. He let go of her hand, then looked down at the table. "I haven't seen them in quite some time," he finally said, not really confirming her earlier statement.

Interesting.

They sat in silence for several minutes as he gave her time to wrangle her emotions under control. Chiara appreciated it, she really did, but at the same time she wanted badly to have him divulge a part of him the way she just had.

Eventually, it became clear that just wasn't going to happen. Not tonight, anyway. She forced a smile on her face and popped open the next passing bowl. "This looks good," she commented as she set it down between them on the table.

He pointed at her. "You sure? That's one of the spiciest rolls on the menu."

With a fortifying breath, she picked up one of the pieces. "I guess I'm living dangerously."

He wasn't kidding. Her mouth was burning by the time she swallowed. For his part, Evan appeared barely affected after swallowing his share in one bite.

"I tried to warn you."

"You didn't try very hard," she countered with a grimace as the pain of her burning tongue started to slowly subside.

Evan signaled for more water and soon she was ready to try again.

"How many plates has that been?" she asked, beginning to feel rather full. "Dozens?"

He laughed, lifting the latest empty one. "This is number twenty." He slipped it into the slot. "Watch this."

The anime cartoon on the tablet above them began to dance and sing. Then an array of fireworks played on the screen. A clear plastic tube by the side of the table started to vibrate. Then a small plastic round ball dropped through it and into Evan's hand where he held it below the tube.

He handed it to her. "For you. In honor of your first *kaitenzushi*."

"A prize?"

"Yep. Diners get rewarded after every twenty plates."

Chiara was ridiculously amused. She felt like a child who'd just managed to snag something out of one of those arcade claw machines. With a laugh, she took the ball and twisted it open.

Inside was a small plastic Christmas tree ornament meant to be a wrapped present. "Perfect!" she squealed in delight, loud enough to earn a smile from the older couple at the table next to them. "I will cherish it forever."

Evan threw his head back with a peal of laughter. "You're into the finer things in life, I see."

"Oh, yes. Tiny plastic Christmas ornament. I collect them."

He lifted an eyebrow. "Want to try for another? We only need to eat twenty more plates of sushi."

As much as she'd enjoyed the meal, her stomach groaned in protest at the thought. "I'm happy with my winnings for the night," she said and pocketed her tiny present. "Plus, I'm very full."

Evan keyed in a request for the check when Chiara noticed something heading toward them on the conveyor belt that most definitely didn't belong there. She pointed at it. "That's not sushi?"

Evan followed the direction of her finger. "No. It's not. That would be a cell phone."

Huh. That was curious. "Why in the world would someone put their cell phone on the belt?"

"To take video as it goes around."

What a novel idea. Still, it seemed rather risky.

"I've seen it in Japan," Evan said. "Kids like to record video and post it on their social media accounts." He leaned forward over the table. "We'll be polite and give a wave."

She met him in the middle, their heads touching. Both smiled for the camera as the device glided by. Was it her imagination or did Evan linger near her just a bit longer after the cell phone had gone past them and reached the next table? He'd grown some stubble on his chin since this morning, the five o'clock shadow lending a casual ruggedness to his handsome face. For an insane moment, she wanted to turn her head to face him directly, wanted to look straight in his eyes to see what she might find there.

The moment was over before she could decide either way, leaving her to wonder whether she would have been bold enough. And where exactly such boldness may have led.

Within minutes, they'd paid the bill and were back outside. The night had grown darker but no less busy. Crowds of people lined the sidewalk where long lines had formed in front of street food vendors. Bouncy pop music in a language she didn't recognize rang through the air. She

found herself bopping her head to the beat as they began to walk.

"I thought the hotel was the other way?" she asked.

"It is. I thought we might do some sightseeing. If you're up for it, that is."

Oh, she most definitely was. She clapped her hands together in front of her chest. "I would adore that."

He chuckled. "Now, why did I know that would be your answer?"

Which said a lot, didn't it? Somehow this man knew her better than most other people on earth, despite them having met only days ago.

Soon, Chiara found herself approaching what could only be described as a holiday wonderland.

"Oh, my heavens."

Evan paused, letting her just take in the spectacular view.

"What is this place?" she asked, her breath hitching.

"Come on. I'll show you."

He led her by the hand down a path toward the activity. A bridge done up in what had to be thousands of tiny lights served as the entrance. A gondola sat floating beneath, and seated inside was a waving elf and a woman costumed as a princess.

Chiara took her cell phone out to take a video, but she knew there was no way to capture the magic before her digitally. "Wait till Nuri sees these pictures."

"Hope you have a full battery," Evan said. "The Gardens by the Bay Christmas Wonderland goes on for at least a mile."

They walked past the bridge into a kaleidoscope of colorful lights beyond. The towering city buildings above the gardens served as a frame for the overall picture. A Christmas tree in the center of the square sat amidst dozens of tall columns lit up with circular designs atop that reminded her of elaborate dream catchers.

Beyond the square, a merry-go-round turned with children and adults alike riding the statue animals. A portly Santa walked through the surrounding crowd, handing out wrapped presents and treats.

"What do you think so far?" Evan asked as she snapped more photos.

"I don't think I have the right words to answer."

"Does it compare to the holiday season in New York City?"

"Most definitely. But it's very different as well."

He lifted an eyebrow. "Oh? I've been to New

York, of course. Several times. But I'd like a native's point of view for comparison's sake."

Chiara tried to gather her thoughts. Christmas in New York was just something she'd taken for granted growing up. It was her home city, and the holidays was only one of the ways the city changed dynamically through different times. Now that the subject had come up, it surprised her just how much she'd missed being there during the holiday season.

"And this is different?" he asked, gesturing with his chin at the scene before them. "Tell me, what might we be doing if we were in New York right now?"

So many possible answers came to mind. "Maybe watching *The Nutcracker* at the Met. Or taking in all the decorations in Times Square. Or we might attend a Broadway show like *A Christmas Carol*. And there's Rockefeller Center if you wanted to do some ice skating."

She turned to find Evan staring at her with an expression that sent a shiver through her spine. His eyes hooded, his lips slightly pouted.

"Maybe you could show me all that someday."

Her heart skipped a beat. This was the first time he'd so much as hinted at the two of them staying in touch once this AI business was taken care of.

"I'd like that, Evan," she said in a soft voice that sounded foreign to her own ears. But he'd already turned away, as if he regretted the words that had come out of his mouth and wanted to move on quickly.

Their earlier easy and comfortable conversation seemed to have dissipated. Chiara wanted badly to get it back. Waving her arm around at their surroundings, she tried again to answer his earlier question. "This is like if somehow somebody had figured out a way to walk through an array of active fireworks as they lit up the sky. Right amongst the stars."

He laughed at that for some reason. "Then I know exactly where to go next." He draped an arm over her shoulders and began to lead her to the right. It was a casual gesture, Chiara knew. Friendly. Nothing more. But having Evan's arm around her had her blood thrumming through her veins.

"Where?" she asked with fake nonchalance, trying to ignore the electricity that seemed to be crackling between them.

"To walk amongst the stars," he answered.

A few minutes later, Chiara understood what he'd meant. He'd taken her to an open-air tunnel glowing with tiny blue lights shaped like stars. The pathway beneath their feet leading into and through the tunnel was lit up the same way.

As they began to move through the tunnel, Chiara felt as if she'd somehow been lifted into the sky during a starlit night. Evan still held her about the shoulders.

This was going to be a moment she'd remember and cherish forever. Such experiences seemed to be adding up. The thought was bittersweet. For she had no idea what it was going to mean for her psyche long-term. Or her relationships for that matter. What man was ever going to be able to compete when he tried to show her a good time?

A small child brushed past them, giggling and skipping through the tunnel, and pulled Chiara out of her thoughts.

Here and now. She would focus on the moment at hand and not let one second of it go to waste.

When they reached the end of the tunnel, Evan gave her a knowing look. She didn't even need to say anything. He knew exactly what she was thinking. "You want to go through it again, don't you?" he asked.

They walked through the tunnel twice more before she was ready to move on.

An enticing aroma tempted her nose as they walked back toward the square. Something sugary sweet and fruity. Again, Evan seemed to read her mind.

"I know you said you were full after dinner, but there's a row of food vendors that way. Lots of them serve dessert."

Chiara patted her middle. "I always have room for dessert."

The choices were plentiful when they reached the food area. Each one more tempting than the last. The longest line seemed to be at the ice-cream hut. Chiara figured that was as good a way as any to make the decision.

Once they'd gotten their ice cream, Evan found them an empty bench to sit. As much as she wanted to keep snapping pictures to send to Nuri, Chiara desired more to simply take in all the views before her. And to enjoy Evan's company undistracted. Ha. She could laugh at that. As if she could forget for even one instant who she was seated with and the growing effect he seemed to be having on her emotions.

An older couple walking past smiled at them, then paused directly in front of their bench. Evan's response was a respectful nod with a slight bow. Chiara had no idea what to do so she followed his lead and mimicked the action.

But they didn't move on.

The woman pointed to the top of the pole behind the bench and said something Chiara didn't understand. Then she nodded enthusiastically. Chiara shrugged her shoulders and gave the woman a smile in return. Why hadn't she thought to learn a few words of greeting in Mandarin before coming to Singapore? Most of Singapore spoke English but it couldn't have hurt to learn a bit of the second most popular language here. Things had just moved so quickly after she'd yes to Evan's offer. In fact, time seemed to be speeding by since the day she'd met him. She leaned sideways in Evan's direction. "What's she saying?"

He turned to her. Their faces were inches apart. "She's pointing out that we happen to be sitting under some mistletoe."

Oh, dear. The couple was still staring at them expectedly. Chiara froze in her spot, at a complete loss as to what to do.

But then Evan lifted her chin with one finger. Suddenly, despite the chaotic fun and boisterous noise surrounding them, Chiara's entire focus narrowed to just the two of them. She gripped the cone in her hand so tight it was a wonder it didn't break.

And she almost dropped it when she felt Evan's lips on hers. Soft yet firm, gentle yet somehow demanding in equal measure. She had no idea if he'd meant to deliver a small peck on the lips in response to a stranger's prompting, but this kiss was quickly turning into so much more than that. Heat and desire curled through her stomach as his mouth remained on hers. Every cell of her being vibrated with desire.

When she finally made herself pull away, she had to take a deep breath to try to regain some of her senses. The older couple wasn't even there any longer.

At some point, their fake kiss had become all too real. For her, anyway. Maybe even for Evan.

CHAPTER EIGHT

WHAT HAD HE been thinking?

It was midnight by the time they made it back to their hotel suite, but Evan was still silently cursing himself.

He hadn't been thinking at all. That was the problem. Kissing Chiara should have never been in the cards. How many times had he reminded himself throughout the night that he had to ignore his attraction to her?

In his defense, that had become increasingly difficult as the evening wore on. He couldn't recall the last time he'd enjoyed himself quite so much in the company of a woman. The way she'd enjoyed herself at the sushi restaurant. Her utter delight at her prize of a tiny piece of plastic. Her excitement at the Christmas Wonderland. He'd been growing more and more intrigued by her sheer magnitude for enjoying life.

Still, he'd managed to hold strong for the most part by reminding himself repeatedly that she was essentially only here as his employee. Until fate had intervened in the form of an older observant couple, as well as a sprig of mistletoe. The woman must have thought he and Chiara were together.

None of it could excuse kissing her. Now he had to try to rectify the situation. He had to somehow regain his sense of camaraderie and easy friendship they'd been enjoying until the ill-fated kiss.

And he had to do it before Louis's wedding. The two of them had to be absolutely convincing at the ceremony and following celebration. At some point, they would have to clear the air about the way he'd kissed her. But it was going to have to wait until the morning.

Because right now he had another awkward scenario to address. When his assistant had booked this stay for him weeks ago, there'd been no need to ask for an extra room or a suite with more than one bed.

Chances of there being any empty units in a hotel like this at Christmas time were slim to none. More poor planning on his part.

Plus, how would he explain that if it ever came up later?

There was nothing for it—he would have to sleep on the couch.

As if on cue, Chiara covered her mouth with

her hand to suppress a wide breathy yawn. "I think I'm ready to call it a day. Is it okay to grab the extra blanket and pillow from the bedroom?"

Confusion washed through him. Was she seriously assuming that she'd be the one sleeping out here? What kind of a guy did she think he was?

"What do you mean?" he asked.

She chuckled at the question. "I mean I'm ready to go to bed. Aren't you?" She gasped and squeezed her eyes shut. "I mean, in your bedroom. You, that is," she quickly corrected. "I'd be out here, of course." She motioned to the couch. "If I could just grab that pillow and blanket."

Before she could take more than one step in the direction of the bedroom, Evan stopped her with a hand to her arm.

"I'll get them." She blinked up at him in confusion. He hadn't meant to sound so brisk. He was just so thrown off by her unquestioning assumption that she'd be the one to sleep on the couch.

She gave her head a vehement shake. "Oh, no. Absolutely not. This is your suite. You're paying for it. I can't be the one to take the only room."

Her voice was hard and determined. She sounded offended, as if he'd insulted her. Well, they were at a bit of a standoff, then. Because he felt rather offended at the idea that he'd let her sleep on a lumpy couch. As expensive and posh as it was, it was no mattress.

"Listen, Chiara. I've slept on much worse."

She held up her hands before he could continue. Then, before he could guess what she was doing, she walked to the center of the room, plopped down on the couch and lay back. "I refuse to leave this sofa," she declared. Grabbing one of the furry cushions, she placed it under her head. "Perfect. I could use a blanket, though."

"Chiara, I can't—"

In a dramatic gesture that bordered on comical, she turned her head and closed her eyes. Then she pretended to snore. Loudly.

Evan fought between laughing at his predicament and swearing out loud. The woman was as stubborn as the black tabby cat he'd had as a child. The one who refused to eat unless it was hand fed, no matter how hungry it got.

He pinched the bridge of his nose, then went to retrieve the blanket and a real pillow. Chiara's eyes were still closed when he came back. He nudged the pillow under her head and removed the cushion, then draped the blanket over her. The obstinate woman didn't so much as open her eyes to look at him. Several beats passed where he just looked at her. Of course, she hadn't fallen asleep this quickly. She had to know he was staring. But he couldn't turn away. Partly to wait her out to see if she might change her mind. And partly because he enjoyed just looking at her.

Delicate cheekbones beneath thick dark lashes. Her wavy hair disheveled and loose after the busy day they'd had. She was beautiful in a way he wouldn't have normally described beauty. If he were a man who wrote poetry rather than code, he could write verses and verses about Chiara Pearson.

Wow. That was a rather fanciful thought.

As much as he hated leaving her out here, he had to walk away.

"Thank you," she called out to his retrieving back when he finally turned in the direction of the bedroom.

Two hours later, it wasn't any kind of surprise that he couldn't sleep. He'd been tossing and turning for most of that time.

This was ridiculous. He just couldn't do it. It wasn't in his DNA to leave Chiara out there while he slumbered in a massive, luxurious bed under a thick down comforter.

Walking back out to the lounge area, he approached the sofa where Chiara lay breathing steadily. She'd kicked off her covers and he could see she'd changed into a tank and a loose pair of running shorts. He didn't want to startle her, so he whispered her name. She roused just enough to offer a sleepy "Hmm?" in response.

"It's just me," he told her, his voice low. Slowly, gently, he picked her up and carried her to the bed. After settling her on the mattress and covering her with the blanket, he turned to make his way to the empty couch.

She grabbed his hand before he could take a step. "Stay."

Evan stood frozen with indecision. Her word was clear, but she was also barely awake. He didn't want to make any kind of presumptuous error here.

"Evan, please. It's a very big bed. There's no need for you to leave."

She had a point. The bed was ginormous. They didn't even need to so much as come in physical contact with each other. And he could definitely use the rest before the spectacle of the big wedding tomorrow. With a sigh, he walked to the other side of the mattress and crawled in. See, no problem. There was at least three feet of mattress between them.

But when he awoke the next morning, Chiara was snuggled tight against his chest, sound asleep, his arms wrapped around her waist.

* * *

Chiara awoke with a start as soon as she felt Evan shift next to her. Thing was, she shouldn't have felt him at all. Somehow, they'd ended up not only side by side, but she was actually wrapped in his arms.

Slowly opening her eyes, she took in her surroundings. She wasn't on the side of the bed he'd placed her in last night. So she'd been the one who'd breached the distance and moved over towards him in her sleep.

How utterly mortifying. Was he awake? If not, maybe she could salvage what was left of her pride and sneak out without him any the wiser about their proximity to each other. And which of them had most likely initiated the closeness. But how in the world was she going to remove herself from his arms?

For one insane moment, she wanted to pretend she hadn't woken up, either. To have an excuse to remain exactly where she was, cocooned in Evan's warmth, his bare chest tight against her back and his strong arms wrapped loosely around her. His hot breath at the bottom of her neck.

Moot point. No such luck. She heard him clear his throat before he spoke. "Chiara? You awake?"

The temptation to lie almost won over. Almost.

"Just woke up. Good morning," she added, though it sounded like a question.

"Good morning," he answered and then, in what had to be the most awkward three or four seconds of her life, unwrapped his arms from around her waist. "I'll go order us some breakfast. We'll have to get ready in a few short hours. Pastries okay?"

She could only nod and stare at him where he stood, wearing only loose-fitting pajama bottoms that looked like they'd been tailored for him. It had never occurred to her that pajamas could be custom-made.

"Pastries sound great. Coffee, too, please."

"That's a given," he threw over his shoulder before walking out of the room.

Huh. Was that it, then?

Between the mind-blowing kiss last night, then waking up like a honeymooning couple, maybe they needed to talk. But she certainly wasn't going to be the one to broach the subject. She wouldn't even know where to start.

Chiara took her time lingering in bed under the covers. Not only because this had to be the most comfortable bed she'd ever lain in, but also to try and assemble her jumbling mess of emotions into some sort of sensical order. She and Evan were clearly attracted to each other. It was going to be a long two weeks if they didn't somehow acknowledge that reality. In fact, she felt more drawn to him than any other man she'd ever encountered.

A disquieting thought slithered into her brain. What if the attraction was completely one-sided? Maybe that's why Evan had hightailed it out of the bedroom just now. Because she'd made him uncomfortable by scooching over to his side. She threw her forearm over her eyes.

But the kiss. She certainly hadn't been the one to trigger that. Evan had been the one to kiss her. He'd had a legitimate reason, an annoying voice told her in her mind's ear. He was simply humoring a sweet older couple who'd noticed they were sitting under mistletoe. The kiss might not have even gone past a peck if she hadn't responded as enthusiastically as she had.

Chiara groaned with mortification and took several steadying breaths. Finally, the smell of freshly brewed coffee had her tempted enough to summon the fortitude to go face Evan.

She found him at the dining counter setting up breakfast. At least he wasn't shirtless this time. She couldn't guess when he'd done so, but at some point he'd put on a tight-fitting cotton T-shirt that looked whiter than first snow.

Too bad it was only slightly helpful that he was fully dressed. The contours of his muscular chest and upper arms were still prominent enough to be distracting. She'd been nestled up tight against those muscles just a few short minutes ago.

"Perfect timing," he told her. "Room service delivery just left." He pointed to one of the dishes. "I know we said pastries, but I took the liberty of ordering you soft-cooked eggs and toast."

She inhaled deeply the savory aromas wafting through the air. "Smells scrumptious. Thank you." The man knew what she wanted better than she did.

He poured her steaming coffee and handed her the mug while she settled onto one of the stools.

After a large gulp of coffee to help summon her nerve, she cleared her throat. "Um… and thank you also for…uh, you know, sharing your bed." Dear saints, could she possibly sound more awkward?

He shrugged. "You were right. It's a large bed. We're both adults."

"Still. It was nice of you to come get me."

Evan grabbed a fork and started in on his own food. "You're welcome."

Now came the hard part. "I just wanted to explain. I'm something of a snuggler."

He swallowed and stared at her. "Snuggler?"

"When I sleep. I like to snuggle with something. At home, I sleep with a really large teddy bear."

He lifted one eyebrow. "Huh?"

"So that's what happened last night," she finished abruptly.

"I see."

An uncomfortable silence hung in the air. Great. In her effort to explain herself, she'd only made things more awkward. She had to change the subject.

"I'm very excited to meet your friends at the wedding." That wasn't entirely true. Actually, the statement was mostly a lie. *Excited* was definitely not the right word to describe the way she felt about the wedding. *Anxious. Terrified. Nervous.* Those were more appropriate.

"And your parents," she added. Another lie.

The way Evan's facial features tightened gave her the impression the change of subject hadn't helped the former awkwardness. In fact, it had somehow intensified. The space between them now practically crackled with tension.

"Look," he began, cramming his fingers through his hair. "There's something you should know."

The muscles above her stomach clenched with dread. What hadn't he told her?

"The truth is my parents and I haven't spoken much over the past few years."

That's it? She could certainly relate. Her desire to travel had kept her from seeing her father or brother for over two years. But she'd spoken to one or both of them nearly daily. She got the impression Evan couldn't say the same about his mother or father. If he had any siblings, she had to think he would have mentioned them by now.

"Oh. Is it because you were too busy launching your app and companies?"

He swallowed with a nod. "Something like that."

"You must be looking forward to seeing them, then."

Evan remained silent.

"Right?" she prodded.

Still no answer. Instead, he glanced at his watch. "I've gotten used to not seeing my parents. They haven't been in my life for several years now."

Chiara couldn't imagine what he was describing. How did anyone grow estranged from their parents to such a degree? She longed for so much as another hour with her mother.

"Did something happen to cause the rift?" Perhaps it was none of her business, but as his faux fiancée, she had to know a few details. What was she supposed to say if the subject came up?

He shrugged. "We were never particularly close to begin with."

"Not even when you were a little boy?"

A flinch of pain seemed to cross his features before he shook his head. "No. I was mostly tended to by nannies and other caretakers." His answers were so matter of fact, as if he were just rattling off data of some sort. But her heart was breaking for the small boy who'd had to grow up with such cold and distant parents.

The wedding was in a few short hours. She really didn't want to walk into something like that, blind about the social dynamics.

"But that's the overall gist of the situation. There's really not much more to explain," he assured her. Something told her that couldn't be quite true. There had to be more there. Evan just didn't seem to want to talk about it. "You're all caught up," he added.

Maybe. But would she have enough time to prepare herself to act accordingly? It sounded like there was some kind of unresolved issue between Evan and his parents. That was sure to make for some uncomfortable encounters between them.

And she'd be right there in the middle.

Evan glanced at his watch, clearly indicating the conversation was over as far as he was concerned. "Anyway, I have an appointment.

I'm just going to hop in the shower, then it's all yours. Enjoy your breakfast."

"Thanks. I will," she said as he strode to the bedroom without so much as a glance behind. Yet another lie. As she seemed to have lost her appetite.

She'd compared him to a teddy bear.

Evan left the revolving door of the hotel lobby and walked out onto the sidewalk. He wasn't sure how his ego was supposed to take that, being compared to a large stuffed animal. When he'd awakened last night to find Chiara had moved over to his side of the bed and nestled herself up against his length, his first reaction wasn't one he was proud of.

He'd been ready to leave the room to go sleep on the couch like he'd first intended. But then she'd tucked her head under his chin, shimmied closer against his body. And suddenly there was more than temptation running through his blood. Comfort. Complete and total comfort.

He couldn't recall the last time he'd felt that way. Not since losing his beloved amah at the age of eleven. The memory of that volatile day sent a shudder through him before the familiar wave of sadness he always felt when he thought of her. He usually avoided such travels down memory lane. But the conversation earlier with

Chiara about his parents had brought all sorts of buried ghosts to the surface.

A few feet away from his intended destination, his cell phone vibrated in his pocket. A smile creased his lips when he saw the contact photo on his screen.

Stopping mid-stride, he clicked to answer. "This is quite an honor," he said into the tiny speaker. "To have a man call you on the day of his wedding… Shouldn't you be rehearsing your vows or something?"

He heard Louis chuckle before answering. "Just thought I'd check in. You know you would have been my best man if I didn't have a twin brother."

"And I would have been honored. Sorry about missing the bachelor parties. There's a lot going on."

"No worries. But you know I'm going to have you make that up to me."

"Name the time and place," Evan said with a laugh. He'd expected nothing less. "How's your beautiful bride? Any last-minute jitters?"

"Who? Gemma? No way. The woman performs for thousands of people on a regular basis. This will be a walk in the park for her."

"You're a lucky man."

"Don't I know it. She mentioned you just last night."

"Oh, yeah? How so?"

"Her manager's daughter will be at the wedding. Solo. We thought—"

"Hold on right there, brother," Evan interrupted before Louis wasted any kind of effort explaining a potential setup for him.

Louis's laugh sounded through the phone. "Let me finish. You can't stay a bachelor forever."

"That's not it, man." Things had moved so fast he hadn't had a chance to update Louis about bringing a plus-one to the wedding. Besides, his friend was rather busy with his upcoming nuptials. He could only hope Louis would be convinced when Evan delivered the news. It wasn't going to be easy; the other man knew him too well. "There's something I need to tell you."

CHAPTER NINE

Did she look the part?

Chiara studied herself in the mirror and took a deep breath to calm her shredded nerves. The delicate silk dress with lace trim clung to her in all the right places. The color seemed to flatter her skin tone. She'd done her hair up in a loose bun that was just formal enough for a high-society wedding outdoors. She hoped so, anyway.

Did she portray what she'd be pretending at later? Is this what the fiancée of a world-renowned tech pioneer might look like at a wedding?

A knock on the bedroom door told her it was much too late to second-guess any of it now. It was time.

"Yes?" she answered. Evan poked his head through the partially open door. "Can I come in? If you're ready?"

She spread her arms out wide. "As ready as I'm going to be."

He walked in and she sucked in a breath at the sight of him. Clad in a tailored tuxedo, he looked like something out of a spy movie. Only he was real. And devastatingly handsome. The dark color of the tux brought out the ebony-black of his eyes. Cleanly shaved, his hair so dark it nearly shimmered, he looked every bit the international success that he was.

Looking into those eyes now, the expression in them as he studied her had her breath hitching in her throat.

"Wow," he finally said after several tense moments. "You look stunning."

Those words combined with the look in his eyes had her stomach clenching in a knot. She may not have had much experience with the opposite sex, but she knew male appreciation when she saw it. Whatever it was that was between them at the moment, she wouldn't have even been able to try to define it. But she had no doubt that if she made any kind of move right now, acted on her attraction in any way, Evan would respond in kind.

The mere thought had heat rushing to her cheeks.

For his part, Evan continued to stare at her, without so much as a blink. For an insane moment, her temptation had her thinking all sorts of impossible thoughts. Like maybe she should act on her desires? Would it be so bad if she stepped toward him, lifted her head up to meet his? Would he kiss her?

Finally, he cleared his throat and looked down. The moment had passed. Relief and disappointment warred within her. She had no idea if she might have gone through with it.

"So, the reason I ran out earlier was to get this," Evan interrupted her confusing thoughts and reached in the pocket of his pants. He pulled out a small black velvet box. "We are engaged, after all."

Her breath caught in her throat as her brain processed what was about to happen. A man was about to give her an engagement ring. But it was all fake. Phony. She wasn't really Evan's fiancée. The moment meant nothing. Not to Evan, anyway.

Still, her breath hitched when he popped open the lid. On a bed of white silk fabric sat a delicate platinum band and a large emerald cut diamond nestled between a pair of blue-sapphire gems. It was the absolute most beautiful piece of jewelry she'd ever laid eyes.

"Might be a little tight," Evan said. "I figured I'd err on the side of too small."

Her voice seemed to have left her. For several moments, she could do nothing but stare at the work of art he'd just presented her with.

"That was smart," she finally replied, hardly hearing her own words over the pounding in her head. "But how?" When had he managed to order a custom ring?

He shrugged. "I asked to have it made ASAP. As soon as you said yes back in Bali."

He must have paid a fortune. Not only for the ring but for the timing. Silently, Evan reached for her left hand and lifted it. Her mind narrowed to the scene before her. Nothing else matter. Evan slipping the ring on her finger, the way his large masculine hand looked holding her smaller one, the glimmer of the three stones. If she allowed her mind to leap, she could easily convince herself that this was all really happening. That this dynamic, exciting, handsome man had really proposed to her, and they were about to embark on a life together as a married couple. That he was, indeed, in love with her. As much as she was with him.

Dear saints, she had it bad, didn't she?

Chiara gave her head a brisk shake. She had to snap out of it. Evan had simply presented her with a piece of a costume. Sure, he'd put some thought into what he'd asked for, considering the color of her eyes. But in the end, it was simply another smart decision made by a very smart man in order to further sell the facade.

"We should go," he told her, guiding her

gently by the hand. "The helicopter should be on the roof waiting."

Helicopter?

"You might want to grab a scarf," he said, pointing at her head. "For your hair. It can get windy in those things."

"We're flying to the wedding?"

He gave her mischievous smile. "We can't very well swim there."

She tilted her head. "Evan."

The smile grew. "Oh, didn't I tell you? The ceremony and celebration are being held on a small island off the coast, a few miles away."

Sure enough, when they reached the top of the building, she could hear the loud roar of an engine. A short flight of stairs led them to the roof where a sleek-looking, shiny black helicopter awaited them.

Chiara felt like she could be filming a scene from a spy movie.

Evan handed her a pair of large ear protectors as they climbed aboard. He said something she didn't understand to the pilot and soon they were rising into the air.

Chiara clung to the seat, excitement sending adrenaline shooting through her blood stream. Soaring above the hotel and the other towering buildings, she couldn't even decide where to focus her gaze. The view below her looked like some kind of dynamic painting. To her left, she could the Christmas Wonderland they'd visited just yesterday. Soon, they were above the lion-head statue majestically sprouting a heavy stream of water. The Singapore Flyer observation wheel made for an imposing figure that towered over everything else. She'd have to ask Evan if they might visit the attraction at some point so she could take in the view from the sky just once more before leaving the city.

The water shimmered like painted glass when they reached the air above the shore.

She glanced over where he was seated across from her to see if he was as enchanted by the sights as she was. To her surprise, he wasn't looking down. Rather he was staring right at *her* instead. And heaven help her, the look in in his eyes reminded her of the way he'd looked at her earlier in the bedroom. She had to remind herself to breath.

He lifted his hand and made a motion that mimicked taking a picture. It was too loud to try to explain that she wasn't going to bother, there was no need to pull her cell phone out to try and capture the moment.

She'd been taking so many pictures and videos because she hadn't wanted to risk forgetting even one small detail about this trip. But she'd never forget any bit of this.

Years after she and Evan bid their goodbyes and she returned to her familiar life back in New York, this memory would be a highlight of her life that stayed with her forever.

He couldn't seem to take his eyes off her.

Evan realized he wasn't the only one as they made their way from the beach toward the crowd that had already formed in front of a tall waterfall surrounded by tropical trees and shrubs. The helicopter had landed about a half mile away from where the ceremony would be held. A two-person buggy driven by a tuxedoed driver had taken them the rest of the way.

Louis and Gemma had gone all out. He would have to take notes for when—

Whoa. Where had that thought come from? He wasn't going to need notes about any kind of wedding reception anytime soon. He just wasn't meant for any sort of real relationship. He couldn't even make peace with the two people who had brought him into the world. The only other person he'd ever grown close to… Well, she was gone for good.

He liked his solitary life just fine. He just had to pretend otherwise until he got the signatures on the dotted line.

First, though, he had to get through this wedding. And he had to play the part of a besotted man in love. Glancing at Chiara walking beside him, he had to admit the act might be easier than he would have expected. He hadn't been exaggerating when he'd told her she looked stunning. The silky wrap dress she wore brought out the dazzling color of her eyes. The fabric clung to her in all the right places. Her hair was done up in some complicated style that somehow looked both elegant and loose. His fingers itched to loosen the ribbon tie and run his fingers down every strand. Then he could proceed to slip the thin straps off her shoulders and lower her dress.

Just. Stop.

He certainly sounded besotted, didn't he?

He couldn't begin to explain what might be wrong with him. It had to be the unusual circumstances he and Chiara were in that had him behaving so uncharacteristically. Slipping an engagement ring on a woman's finger before accompanying her to a romantic wedding would have a disarming effect on any man.

He was only human, after all.

They were approaching the seating area with chairs set up in front of a small waterfall when he heard his name called out from behind. He knew that voice well.

If it wasn't the groom himself.

He turned to find Louis striding toward them. The other man reached their side in seconds and Evan couldn't even be sure which one of them initiated the hug.

"Don't you have somewhere to be?" Evan asked, teasing his dearest friend. "What are you doing out here?"

"I had to see for myself who finally managed to pull this man away from his computer servers." He leaned toward Chiara and jokingly spoke in a quiet voice, his hand hiding both their faces. "You sure you know what you're getting into?"

Chiara answered with a laugh and reached her hand out. "I think so. It's very nice to meet you, Louis. Congratulations."

"Thanks for coming. I hope you enjoy yourself." He gave Evan a useless shove on the shoulder. "You, too. And I want to hear all about how you managed to snare this fine lady."

"Hey, don't go putting doubts in her head now. Also, don't you have to be somewhere? Like the altar?"

"I had to come out here and see for myself. But you're right." He pointed with finger guns at Evan's chest. "We are absolutely catching up during the reception. You two will be at the head table."

With that, Louis turned on his heel and hurried back in the direction he'd come from.

"That was clearly a display of nervous energy just now," Evan said, watching his friend's retreating back. "Don't let his casual demeanor fool you. He's nervous as…well, as a man about to say his vows in front of hundreds of people. He needed a distraction."

"You certainly provided him with one. Bringing an unknown fiancée to his wedding."

Evan chuckled. "I guess I did."

"You know him pretty well."

Better than most anyone else. Evan didn't know what he would have done without Louis's friendship over the years. He'd have to tell Chiara about it someday, all their shenanigans and troublemaking during uni. The time they'd set off unsanctioned fireworks on the roof of their dorm building.

"Known him since we were tots," he answered, then led her toward the seating area, greeting several acquaintances along the way with an acknowledging nod. Not surprisingly, he found his name printed on placards on two wooden chairs in the front row, close to the waterfall.

"Oh, my," Chiara said breathlessly next to him. "What an absolute beautiful setting for a wedding."

"Gemma is the one responsible, I'm guessing. Louis would have been happy to elope in Maui or even Vegas, I'm sure." Though Louis's parents would have been horrified if their son had taken that route. So his friend hadn't even considered that option. Louis was the prodigal son in every way. Unlike Evan himself.

Speaking of which, Evan tensed where he sat in his seat. He felt their presence before he saw them. The very air he was breathing seemed to change and grow thicker, a heaviness settling around his shoulders.

His eyes found them immediately, taking their seats in the first row at the opposite end to where he and Chiara sat.

His mother and father had just arrived.

Chiara felt Evan's whole body go stiff sitting next to her.

In one instant, he had gone from relaxed and carefree to rigid and tense. She wasn't going to get a chance to ask him about it, though, because a string quartet standing next to the podium began to play.

Evan's friend Louis appeared with another man who looked remarkably like him except he'd dyed the tips of his hair to a blonder color. Together, they stood to the side of the podium.

Chiara studied the area around the pond, trying to determine exactly where the bride would appear. There didn't seem to be any kind of pathway on either side of the waterfall. How would anyone, let alone a bride in any kind of gown or heels be able to walk through all that sand?

Then she saw it.

Chiara's jaw fell open when she noticed the vertical haze of white behind the waterfall. A moment later, the very water itself parted down the middle, like stage curtains drawing to the sides. The crowd erupted in applause and a chorus of oohs and aahs. The bride stepped forward, holding the hand of an older gentleman with silver hair wearing a white tuxedo. Together, they stepped out of the cave behind the waterfall and walked down slabs of stone. A rock pathway led them to the podium. There, Louis nodded to the older gentleman and took the bride's hand.

"Wow," Chiara whispered in Evan's ear. "I've never seen anything like that. It must have taken meticulous planning." And cost a fortune, she added to herself. Suddenly, she felt odd and out of place. What was she doing here? These people who surrounded her now had the type of wealth and resources to manipulate actual waterfalls. Her family had been successful enough back in New York. But this was a completely different stratosphere.

Chiara mentally hit pause and took a deep breath.

She could do this. She could play the part she'd been hired to play. Not like she could turn back now in any case.

The ceremony was heartfelt and touching. Despite being the center of attention, Louis and his bride seemed to have eyes for only each other. The love they shared glowed like a tangible aura between their bodies. Chiara felt herself sigh. Would she ever have that? A love that was clearly all-encompassing? Would a man ever look at her the way Louis was looking at his now-wife?

Did she even want it, though? She thought of how heartbroken and shattered her father had been after he'd lost the love of his life. There'd been days when she'd been convinced he might never recover. Did she want to risk that kind of heartbreak for herself?

Her gaze slowly shifted to Evan sitting next to her. His facial features were much softer, some of the tension seemed to have left his shoulders, and he'd shifted lower in his seat. Whatever had caused the earlier tenseness she'd sensed in him appeared to have been lessened somewhat. The ceremony must have had some kind of effect on him also.

What kind of wedding vows might Evan come up with to say to his beloved?

She squeezed her eyes shut and pushed the question out of her mind. She had no business wondering such things about the man. Hadn't she just seen proof of how mismatched they were in terms of economic status? Evan was nothing more than a temporary blip in her life. A man who had simply come up with a way to help her make it back home for the holidays.

Once she handed the ring on her finger back to him in a few short weeks, she'd best forget he even existed.

Right. As if Evan Kim was a man who could be easily forgotten, if at all.

When she reopened her eyes, it startled her to find Evan staring at her. A flush of heat crept into her cheeks. Had he somehow guessed where her mind had led her just now? It was a mortifying thought and she made herself look away before she could meet his eyes fully.

To her further surprise, he reached for her hand and pulled it onto his lap. Chiara's breath caught in her throat at his unexpected touch. Heat shimmied up her spine. Evan tilted his head to the right, indicating the woman sitting a few seats away, gawking at them.

Chiara wanted to kick herself for her foolishness. The way she'd reacted to his touch just now was downright silly. The gesture to hold her hand was just that, a gesture. Merely for show. Whoever this woman was, Evan wanted to convince her he had a fiancée.

She'd been a fool to think otherwise for even a moment.

CHAPTER TEN

CHIARA CLAPPED AND cheered as loud as everyone else around her as the couple kissed after their vows.

She felt like she'd just watched something out of a fairytale. In fact, she felt as if she'd somehow stepped into a fairy tale.

Evan gently nudged her shoulder with his own. "Come on. Now, we eat. I'm starved."

The woman who'd been staring at them during the ceremony approached before they got past the seating area. "Evan. It's been so long. How have you been, dear?" She didn't wait for an answer before turning to Chiara. "And who might this be?" she asked.

Evan greeted the woman with a large smile. "Nice to see you, Marylin. Allow me to introduce my fiancée. This is Chiara Pearson. From New York City."

If the other woman was taken aback at all by the announcement, she didn't show it. Marylin shook her hand, somehow barely touching it to do so.

"Pleasure to meet you," Chiara said politely.

"Congratulations," she addressed both of them. "I'm so happy for you."

Chiara had no idea how genuine the statement was. The woman was impossible to read.

"Marylin is head of global acquisitions for Fruitland," Evan explained.

Whoa. That was a major platform to download practically every app in existence. No wonder Evan had pulled the little handholding act back there. The people Evan was hoping to convince were here and they had noticed.

Time to put her game face on.

"Chiara's family owns the Grand York hotel chain, which is based in New York. We met when she served as a translator for me during a business meeting."

Of course, he would introduce her that way. And not as the hotel housekeeper he'd met only days ago. But rather as some kind of hotel heiress. Which, technically, she supposed she was. The truth was she hadn't really been active or involved with the family business. It had hurt too much after the loss of her mother. Just walking into the Grand York's lobby brought back too many memories of the days they'd spent there together as a family.

Marylin congratulated them once more before moving on. Evan was then stopped by several other people as they made their way through the crowd and Chiara's face muscles started to grow strained from all the smiling as he introduced her to everyone who approached. Shock at the news of his engagement seemed to be the general reaction.

Finally, they reached the head table where the bride and groom had just begun to take their seats. Louis immediately abandoned his chair and reached their side.

"Chiara, come let me introduce you to my bride," he said, taking her lower arm and leading her to the center of the table. Evan followed close on her heels.

After he made the introductions, Chiara reached for the woman's hand to shake but found herself in a tight hug instead. "That was quite an entrance!"

Gemma clasped a hand to her chest. "Do you think it was too much?"

Chiara had to laugh at the concern in her voice. "Absolutely not. A girl should be able to make a grand entrance at her own wedding."

Gemma giggled. "I debated and agonized over going through with it." She glanced downward. "I just wanted to take his breath away."

Goal achieved, then. Chiara's own breath had left her at the sight of the bride and her father walking through a waterfall, then over the pond to her intended. "I have no doubt you would have done that no matter how you entered."

The other woman reached for her hand then and took it in hers, giving it a squeeze. "I think we're going to get along marvelously, Chiara Pearson."

A lump formed in her throat. Genuine sentiment shone in the other woman's eyes. Suddenly, she felt small and unworthy. If Gemma only knew that at this very moment Chiara was betraying her with a blatant lie...

And though Chiara had only just met the other woman mere moments ago, it shamed her that she'd already betrayed her trust. She could only hope when all this was over, Gemma and Louis would understand and forgive her.

Not that she would ever know. The chances of her running into a real estate mogul and his classical pianist wife afterward were slim to none. Chiara didn't exactly run in the same circles. That thought only served to escalate her sadness.

Maybe they'd stay at the Grand York someday. And she could try to explain herself. Chiara would love to get the chance at some point.

A chance to clear her name would mean so much.

Evan watched as various couples gradually made their way to the wooden dance floor built near the water. This was as good a time as any to ramp up their act. A man had to dance with his fiancée, didn't he?

He waited while Chiara took another bite of her crab and shrimp curry. She took her times chewing and swallowing, as if savoring every morsel. The woman certainly seemed to enjoy good food. In fact, it was doing strange things to his libido to watch her eat.

Wasn't that a sorry state of affairs?

In his defense, the way she made a soft moaning sound with each swallow would tempt any man, for more than just food. He had to look away before she took another bite.

Finally, she set her fork down and he leaned toward her and spoke just loud enough in her ear over the loud hip-hop beat of the song the band was playing. Though *band* wasn't quite the right word. Mini orchestra was probably more like it. In addition to the quartet for the ceremony, Louis and Gemma had commissioned another group for the celebration afterward.

"Ready to dance?" he asked.

Her eyes grew wide. For a split second, he thought she was going to turn him down. Instead, she bounced out of her seat. "I thought you'd never ask. They're playing some of my favorite songs."

Evan chuckled at her reaction, then led her off

the dining platform and toward the action on the beach.

"I've never seen such a large band at a wedding," Chiara remarked, following behind him to the dance floor, her hand still clutched in his.

"Gemma knows quite a few musicians, given her line of work."

Her pace faltered a step. "Right. I'd almost forgotten. The bride is a world-renowned classical musician barely in her twenties and one of the guests is the CEO of a major media platform. I'm guessing all the other guests are just as accomplished."

Evan couldn't guess what she was getting at. But he thought better of mentioning the two diplomats in attendance. Not to mention the global status of his own parents.

"Come on," he encouraged her instead as they joined the throngs on the dance floor. "Let me show you my moves."

He playfully twirled her around three times before they started shuffling together to the bouncy music. Chiara's laughter was contagious. He couldn't remember the last time he'd actually enjoyed dancing. If ever.

She leaned in closer. "You know, for a techie, you're not so bad on your feet."

He gave her a mini bow. "I accept your compliment. You're not so bad yourself."

Suddenly, without announcement, the band slipped into a much slower love song, one full of suggestive lyrics. Chiara's eyes darted around the dance floor, then found his, silently asking him what to do. Without thinking, Evan pulled her close to his chest, wrapped his hands above her hips. She stood frozen for the briefest second. Then her arms found their way around his shoulders. For several moments, they simply swayed together.

"This is working great," he whispered in her ear, simply to have something to say. "We've definitely got the right people's attention. And letting Marylin Tamin know we're engaged will go a long way."

For the second time that night, he felt Chiara's steps falter. She stiffened in his arms and pulled away a fraction of an inch. "I'm glad it's working," she said into his shoulder after staying silent so long it surprised him when she spoke.

Half a song later, she stepped out of his arms. "I think that's enough dancing for me, right now. I'm feeling a little thirsty."

Was it his imagination or had her voice hardened somewhat? Probably just tired after all the dancing. He wrapped his arm around her waist. "Let's get you something to drink, then. There are cocktail fountains somewhere."

She shook head. "Maybe just some water for

now. I had a couple of glasses of wine with dinner earlier. I usually pace myself better."

"Don't be too hard on yourself. Louis's dad owns several vineyards in the Loire Valley region in France. That was some of the finest wine bottled within the last century."

Chiara's hand flew to her mouth. "And I gulped it down like cheap bubbly from the corner store. You should have told me."

"Told you to stop drinking your wine with dinner?"

"No. But you might have mentioned how expensive it was. I wouldn't have had so much."

Evan chuckled as he led her away. "Chiara, you need to relax a bit. You're doing great. Everyone thinks we're head over heels—"

He swallowed the last word when the woman appeared in front of him. Dressed in an off-gray silk gown that had to have cost a fortune, she remained silent. Surprising as it was, she hadn't really changed at all since the last time he'd seen her all those years ago, though a few more wrinkles framed her eyes and lips. Hardly noticeable ones. The woman had always been meticulous about taking care of herself with a skin-care routine that could best be described as militant.

Evan blew out a sigh and cursed the timing that had caught him off guard. He wasn't prepared. Had been too preoccupied by the way Chiara had felt in his arms as they danced together. But it was just as well. It wasn't as if he was going to be able to avoid them the whole wedding. May as well get it over with.

"Hello, Mother," he said, fully meeting her gaze. Chiara's gasp was clearly audible next to him.

"Chiara, this is my mother, Luann Kim."

Chiara immediately stepped forward with her hand outstretched. The other woman took it for less than a second before pulling her arm away.

"Mother, this is Chiara Pearson. My fiancée."

"So I've heard."

Chiara felt zero warmth emanating from this woman. None. It was like speaking to an icebox. What was wrong with her? Evan said they hadn't even seen each other for years. And here he was introducing her to his *fiancée*, albeit a fake one. But she didn't know that. Yet, his mother was utterly, astonishingly unmoved in any way.

"I congratulate you on your engagement, then," she added, not sounding congratulatory at all.

"Thank you," Chiara and Evan replied in unison.

"You feel ready to be married then, son." She

said it in a way that sounded like it could be both statement and question.

Evan simply nodded once.

"I hope it works out," Luann said, with a quick glance in Chiara's direction. Chiara could only hope the woman really meant it.

Her next words gave her some kind of clue about how genuine she was. "You certainly don't need to add a failed marriage to your list of life disappointments."

Chiara couldn't believe her ears. What kind of statement was that? To her own son? Barely realizing what she intended, she took a small step forward, partially standing between Luann and Evan. "With all due respect, ma'am, everyone has disappointments and failures. Very few men accomplish all that Evan has at such a young age." Chiara knew she should stop there. But her mouth didn't seem to want to listen to her better judgment. "Most mothers would be proud of all he's done," she added.

For several beats, an awkward silence hung there with only the background noise of the wedding. Oh, dear.

"Hmm… You're from New York, yes?" The words sounded like some sort of accusation.

What was she getting at? "Yes, that's right. Though I'm not sure I understand what that has to do with anything."

Luann lifted her shoulders in a mini shrug "I've heard those from New York are prone to speak their mind. Even things better left unsaid," his mother uttered as her eyes ran the length of Chiara.

"I'm sorry," Chiara repeated, not really meaning it this time. "But I don't agree with that." Some things did, indeed, have to be said.

"I'm sure you don't," the other woman replied. Without so much as another glance, she turned on her heel and walked away.

Chiara's blood ran cold. Her first encounter with Evan's mom and the conversation had not gone well. Maybe Mrs. Kim was right. She should have never said what she had, should have found a way to keep her mouth shut. To make matters worse, there was no doubt there'd been at least a couple people who'd played audience to the display. And she was certain at least one of them had snapped a picture.

What had she been thinking?

Chiara was horrified at what she'd just done. Only, she hadn't been thinking at all, had she? She should have just smiled politely and expressed her pleasure at meeting Evan's mother. She had no excuse. Except that her nerves had just been so frazzled after that slow dance with Evan. The way he had been holding her, swaying with her to the soft melody. The smell of him surrounding her, the warmth of his body against hers. Then to have him throw cold water over her when he'd explained exactly what he was doing.

Playing at the charade he was paying her for.

This was a calamity. The wine probably hadn't helped matters.

She risked a glance at Evan once his mom had walked away. A muscle twitched along his jaw. His chin was set in a rigid hard line, his lips tight.

Probably not a good sign.

She clenched her hands together, willing for him to say something. Anything to let her know how big of a faux pas she'd just committed and if there was anything she could do to rectify it somehow. Should she be chasing his mom down, pleading an apology?

Evan remained silent so long Chiara was close to panic. She would have welcomed the random opening of a sinkhole right where she stood so the earth could swallow her whole.

Finally, when she was certain she wouldn't be able to take another moment, he pivoted on his heel.

"Come on," he said to her over his shoulder. "Let's go get you that water. And I could use a drink myself."

Chiara blinked at his retreating back. That

was it? He wasn't going to even acknowledge what had just happened? He answered that question a moment later when she caught up to him at one of the four bars set behind the stage.

"Let's take a walk," he told her, handing her a sweaty glass bottle of water from a standing ice bucket near the bar, then reaching for a small tumbler half full of amber liquid the server handed him.

Great. This was probably going to be worse than the silent treatment she'd been so worried about just moments ago. Evan was about to read her the riot act. Estranged or not, Chiara had just somehow offended his mother. In front of witnesses. Something told her that sort of thing didn't sit well, particularly in this part of the world.

Evan led them to a couple of wooden Adirondack chairs near the water and deposited his tuxedo jacket over the back of one. Chiara kicked her shoes off, tucking her legs under her as she sat.

"Look, Evan," she began before he could say anything, arguing in advance in her defense. "I know I overstepped back there, and I shouldn't have said what I said, but I want you to know that I meant it all."

He took a generous sip of his drink, his eyes never leaving the horizon. "Chiara, there wasn't any kind of need for you to say anything. We're here portraying an engaged couple so I can finalize a business deal."

Ouch. Pretty matter-of-fact summary. It stung more than she would have liked, enough that she felt the burning of tears behind her eyes. He was telling her to stay out of his personal life. "I see. In other words, I just need to play my little role and not cause any waves."

"That's not what I said."

Maybe not. But it was what he meant. Suddenly, she felt no small amount of anger herself. She was thoroughly out of her element here. She could have used some advanced knowledge of the rift between Evan and his parents before attending the same wedding and coming face-to-face with one of them.

"Maybe you should give me a script so there isn't any more instances of overstepping on my part."

When he finally looked at her, his eyes were hard and cold. Chiara sucked in a deep breath. Despite his relatively mild tone of voice, Evan Kim was beyond annoyed. She might even venture to guess that he was angry.

Yep, she must have really stepped in it this time. No one had probably ever spoken to Mrs. Kim like that in her lifetime. Chiara had really been out of line. She would have to apologize.

Evan would have to guide her on the best way to do that.

Only, Evan's steely profile didn't give her the impression he was ready to talk just yet.

What was she even doing here? The whole situation was surreal. For the first time since they'd left Bali, real doubt and trepidation rose like an evil serpent in the back of her mind. The reality was she had no idea what she was doing.

Damn it. She was not going to cry. The tears would stay unshed no matter how hard she had to fight them. But she couldn't suppress an errant sniffle, which was just loud enough that Evan turned to her. Shock washed over his features, and he cursed out loud.

In an instant, he'd set his tumbler down on the armrest of his chair and he was in front of her.

"Oh, God. Chiara, please don't cry."

His reaction only made her feel worse. She didn't mean to guilt him. It was why she'd tried so hard not to give in to the urge to say something in the first place.

"I'm not crying," she argued.

He swallowed. "That's pretty damn close." He forced his fingers through the hair at his crown. "Look, if it makes you feel better, your delivery was wrong, and you went about it terribly…"

"How is any of that supposed to make me feel better?"

"Because, despite how you went about it, no one's ever stuck up for me like that before. Well, not since several years ago. And then I was just a child."

Chiara sniffled despite herself, dabbed at her eyes with the back of her hand. "Tell me."

"I had a nanny when I was little. She was the one who looked after me as a child. She actually stood up to my parents on my behalf. More than once."

"Do you still stay in touch with her?"

"She's gone. I lost her years ago."

"I'm sorry."

Before he could respond, a group of guests ran onto the beach only a few feet away from where they sat. They had some kind of small rubber ball and started playing an impromptu mini volleyball game without a net. Or the right-sized ball. Dressed in glamorous gowns and tuxes. Despite herself, Chiara found herself distracted and laughing at the sight.

Evan didn't seem as amused. He stood and held his hand out to her. "Come on, let's find a more private spot where we can talk."

She bent forward for her shoes in the sand, but Evan beat her to it and picked them up. As he stood, he reached for her, tucking a strand of wayward hair behind her ear.

Is that real? she couldn't help but think. Was

he simply putting on a show for the volleyballers on the beach? Or did he really want to touch her that way? And what did it mean for her that she had to know for the sake of her heart?

Leading her by the hand, he walked them down yet another stone pathway behind the line of shrubbery. To her surprise, once they cleared the greenery, there appeared rows and rows of small huts. "What is this?" she asked.

"For guests who want to spend the night. Anyone who wants to celebrate into the wee hours."

"Huh." It was all she could think of to say.

"They're equipped with everything. From a complimentary change of clothing to generator electricity."

This was certainly unlike any other wedding she'd ever attended. The ultra-wealthy certainly lived in an entirely different world, didn't they? Fully functional housing huts on the beach for those guests who didn't feel like flying back to shore in private helicopters.

The ever-present question was highlighted yet again. What was she doing here amongst such people?

"We can talk privately in one of them." He took her inside the closest hut and shut the wooden door behind them.

Chiara had to blink to believe her eyes. A fully

made bed sat in the center of the single room. Two robes and various clothing hung on a rack against the wall. A wicker door led to a small restroom on the opposite wall. The place was bigger than her hostel room back in Bali. "This is unbelievable."

"They've been planning this wedding for close to two years," Evan explained, then crossed his arms in front of his chest. "Look, it's my fault what happened out there. I should have warned you to say as little as possible to either of my parents."

Did he really think that was the problem?

"I didn't mean to make you feel uncomfortable at any point during this arrangement we have," he continued.

For several beats, Chiara could only stare, slack-jawed. Then she finally found her voice. "Do you really think that any of those things I said to your mother back there has anything to do with our arrangement? That I might have been playacting or something of the sort?"

He swallowed and nodded, though his expression appeared much less certain than it had seconds ago when he'd made his comment.

"I see. What you really think is that I stuck my nose in where it doesn't belong. That it's really none of my business. Is that right?"

His lips tightened before he spoke. "Chiara."

"Maybe I made it my business because I've grown to care about you!" Chiara actually stomped her foot, and didn't care that it might look like a childish tantrum. "Though, at this moment, I can't exactly say why." She hated that the last word came out in a hiccup. But she was way past her boiling point now.

Suddenly, the very air in the room seemed to have shifted, grown heavy. Evan's eyes darkened. He took a step toward her. "What did you just say?"

Despite his ominous tone, or what it might mean, Chiara decided to hold her ground. She'd made an admission because it was the truth. She would stick with it, not about to backtrack in any way. Heaven help her if that decision proved to be a mistake. "I've grown to care about you, Evan." She pushed her hair off her forehead, not caring that it might mess up her meticulous updo. "I don't even know when it happened. But I hated hearing those things your mother said. Hated that *you* had to hear them."

He reached her in two strides. Before she knew what was happening, his lips were on hers. Her body's response was immediate and fierce. Heat exploded deep in her belly, her blood pounded through her veins, her skin felt aflame from head to toe. Chiara wrapped her arms around his neck and succumbed fully to his kiss, tasting him, inhaling his scent, feeling his warmth.

She'd wondered all her life and now she knew. *This* was what true passion felt like, true desire. The way she wanted this man made her feel alive in ways she couldn't define. She'd felt that desire from that moment on that Bali beach when they'd collided. How in the world had she fought it so long? No more. She'd admitted it now. Both to herself and to Evan. Regret would not enter the picture in any way. No matter what came next.

Evan's hands moved down to her hips, and he pulled her tighter against him. A feminine rush of pleasure washed through her entire being at the contact. He continued the delicious onslaught against her lips. Chiara wanted to melt into him, nothing in the world existed except the man who held her in his arms.

Without warning, he suddenly pulled away, panting and leaving her downright breathless.

"Tell me if you think we should go back to the wedding, Chiara. Right now."

It took several moments for her mind to come back to earth and process what he was asking. Evan was making sure she knew it was her decision.

"Or would you like to stay here. In this cabin?" he asked.

Try to live your life as fully as you can, my dearest. Don't let any moment of happiness pass you by.

Her mom's voice echoed through her head yet again. Surely, this would be one of those moments she must have been referring to.

"I'd like to stay." Her voice sounded thick to her own ears.

Evan closed his eyes tight, tilted his head back. "Chiara, I need to be sure what you're saying here. I don't want to misconstrue anything only to find out I'm terribly wrong."

The man really needed everything laid out in black-and-white, didn't he? Zeros and ones.

Chiara reclaimed the distance between them. She ran her hands along his shoulders until he'd reopened his eyes and focused them back on her face. "I'd like to stay," she repeated. "And seeing as we've already taken over this cabin, I'd like to stay all night."

His enthusiastic response told her just how much he wanted the very same thing.

CHAPTER ELEVEN

Three days later

WELL, THE PLAN was working. It hadn't even taken very long. Evan tossed his tablet onto the sofa and rubbed his eyes. Just as he'd expected, the gossip sites and magazines had taken the bait. He and Chiara were the talk of the tech world. Which meant the private social grapevines were most likely raging with countless messages back and forth about the big mystery surrounding Evan Kim's sudden engagement.

Even their photo from the sushi place in Bali had somehow been found and published. The headline above it read *Tech Wunderkind to Tie the Knot*. With the subheading *Rumor Has it They're Traveling to Beijing Together Next!*

Exactly what he'd intended when he'd made Chiara the offer all those days ago. Now the only question was what exactly was real and what was pretend. So many lines had been blurred the night of Louis and Gemma's wedding. He had to wonder if a few major ones had been crossed.

One thing was certain, he had to try to keep his distance from Chiara as best he could until he figured it all out. Which wasn't going to be easy. Close proximity aside, his attraction to her tempted him like no other woman had before. He'd always prided himself on his unwavering discipline and the strength of his sheer will. Both those traits were taking a serious hit because of Chiara Pearson's effect on him.

The object of his thoughts strode into the room at that very moment, fresh from a long shower. The woman sure enjoyed bathing. That thought had all sorts of unbidden images that he had to push away. She was dressed in dark wool pants and a thick knitted sweater. She wrapped a winter scarf around her neck as she walked past where he sat on the couch.

"Good morning, Evan."

"Morning." Evan stood. "Are you going out?"

She flashed him a brilliant smile full of excitement. "I called the concierge earlier. She mentioned some tours I can join."

"Tours?"

She nodded with enthusiasm. "To see the Great Wall."

Huh. "You want to play tourist?"

She tilted her head. "I've wanted to see it since I was a little girl. My mom used to read me a picture book about an adventurous crow who tried to fly the wall from end to end." Some of the light seemed to fade from her eyes as she spoke. She clasped her hand together. "Anyway, you said you'd be much too busy prepping for your meetings to do any kind of sightseeing."

He had said that, hadn't he? On the flight here to Beijing, he'd made sure to emphasize to her that he wouldn't be able to spend much time with her or away from his desk. He'd almost convinced himself it was really because he had work to do. And not due to the self-preservation instinct that had kicked in after their night together.

"So I looked into ways I could venture out myself," Chiara said.

It made no sense whatsoever, given that the situation was of his own doing, but a sliver of hurt settled in his chest that she hadn't asked him to take her.

Evan thrust his hands into his pants pockets. How silly of him. He should be happy. Chiara was resourceful enough that she'd found a way to entertain herself. Plus, she'd be with a tour group, so he didn't have to worry about her safety out there in an unfamiliar city where she didn't know the language.

So why was he dreading having her walk out the door? Suddenly, the thought of spending hours and hours here, alone in a hotel room without her company, going over line after line of code, had him tempted to hurl his laptop out the window.

While she was out there taking in the sight of the majestic wall for the first time. He could picture her gasping at its beauty while she shivered in the cold. Maybe there'd be a solo American businessman there on the tour with her. Doing some sightseeing himself. He might offer her his scarf. They'd get to talking…

Just stop.

A trail of guilt crept into his chest. Despite the intimate night they'd spent together, he had no claim to her. In fact, he'd been downright insensitive to her wishes. She wanted to see the Great Wall because of a memory tied to her mother. Instead of offering to accompany her to one of the true wonders in the world, he'd shot down the idea before it had even come up.

She studied his face and bit her top lip with her bottom teeth. Why did the woman look so damn sexy when she did that? "Unless… Do you want me to stay here for some reason?"

Evan puffed out a breath. What a loaded question that was. The answer couldn't be denied. He did want her here. With him. And selfish or not, the thought of her being approached by another man made him queasy.

"Evan?" she prompted after several seconds in silence. She glanced at the digital clock above the flat screen. "The tours are due to leave in a short while. I need to get down there if I'm going to hop on to one."

A much too loud voice in his head screamed at him to tell her that her leaving now was the last thing he wanted. The words were on the tip of his tongue.

I want to be the one you see the Great Wall with. I want to hold your hand as you take in the sights. I want to see your expression when you first lay eyes on wonder that attracts millions of people. Instead of random strangers and a monotone tour guide, I want to be the one to tell you about its history. I want to tell you about the many times I visited it myself as a child.

But the words never left his mouth. Instead, he uttered ones he didn't mean. "Yeah. You should definitely get down there before it's too late."

Her shoulders dropped, whether in relief or some other reaction he couldn't be sure of and didn't want to guess.

"Have fun," he said to her retreating back as she grabbed her gear and walked out the door without another word to him.

* * *

She couldn't bring herself to do it. Chiara settled into one of the plush velvet chairs in the lobby and watched the group of tourists follow the smiling guide outside to a sleek, shiny black van. She'd made it all the way downstairs and to the concierge desk and gotten into line before she turned on her heel. As much as she wanted to see the Great Wall, she wasn't sure she could do it surrounded by people she'd never laid eyes on before.

The memory of her mother was already bubbling to the surface of her emotions. Being there without her mom was sure to bring her to tears at some point and she didn't want to be around strangers when that happened. For one insane second upstairs, she thought maybe Evan would change his mind about staying in and offer to accompany her. Instead, he'd practically pushed her out the door. He was probably glad to be rid of her.

And if she thought spending one night in his arms made that unlikely, she should have known better. They'd simply succumbed to their desires. Plus, she'd practically thrown herself at him. Not many men turn down such offers. She'd obviously made more of their intimacy than he had. He'd been nothing but cold and distant since. No wonder he wanted her gone.

Now, she just had to figure out what she was going to do with herself for the day.

Two pots of jasmine tea later, no ideas had materialized. Any kind of tour the hotel offered had already embarked and she was in no mood to wander the streets alone. She also didn't have any kind of money to shop.

One thing was certain, she couldn't drink another drop of tea, as delicious as it was. And she certainly couldn't sit here for hours shuffling through her phone, staring at pictures of an attraction she could have physically visited if only she could have been strong enough to bring herself to do it alone.

Her phone lit up and vibrated where she'd placed it facedown on the coffee table in front of her chair. Her heart leaped with hope. But when she grabbed the device and glanced at the screen, it wasn't Evan's contact icon that greeted her.

Her brother's goofy picture she used as his avatar photo popped up on her screen instead. She hadn't called him in days after telling him she would. She had to answer. Besides, it would kill at least a few minutes.

"Hello—" She'd hardly gotten the word out before Marco interrupted her.

"Hey, sis. Long time, no talk."

"Yeah, sorry about that. I've been kind of busy."

She heard her brother suck in a breath. "Yeah, about that. Anything you want to tell me?"

A queasy feeling curled at the top of her stomach. What was he getting at? "Uh…about?"

Several seconds passed without an answer. She pulled the phone from her ear to see if they'd somehow lost the connection. Marco was still on the line.

"I don't know," he finally said. "Maybe you can explain why my tech friend just called to congratulate me on your upcoming nuptials. He saw a picture of you on some website. It was taken in a restaurant in Singapore. You're seated with a tech world wunderkind billionaire."

Oh, no. She should have been better prepared for this. Marco and Evan may not travel in the same circles, but her brother was a hotelier who knew all sorts of people from various backgrounds and fields of work. Things with Evan had just moved so fast, Chiara hadn't even had time to give much thought to how she'd explain her 'engagement' once word of it reached her sibling. Truth be told, she hadn't expected Marco to catch wind of it quite so soon. She gripped the phone tight in her hand, trying to come up with a response.

Marco continued, "I called up the photo for

myself. Unless you have a doppelgänger, the mystery lady rumored to be engaged to this software mogul appears to be you."

"Marco. Things are…complicated in my life right now." The explanation was so much less than he deserved. But right now, it was all she could give him.

She heard him sigh. "Are you safe? I have contacts all over the world who can be at your side in no time if you need."

An ocean of love and gratitude blossomed in her chest at his concern. She hastened to assuage it. "I'm fine. Really. You absolutely don't need to worry."

"Are you sure?" he pressed.

"Yes. In fact, I'm enjoying tea in the busy lounge of a five-star hotel as we speak. I'll send you a snapshot."

She could almost feel his relief through the tiny phone speaker. "Okay. Then tell me what's going on."

"I can't, Marco. I'm sorry."

"Chiara—"

She didn't let him finish. "Can you just trust me, big bro? I'll explain everything as soon as I can. I know it's a lot to ask."

He uttered a mild curse. "It really is, sis. You're not making things easy on me here."

She closed her eyes and thought what her own

reaction would be if the roles were reversed. No doubt, Chiara would demand to know every detail. But Marco was unlike her in so many ways, despite their shared DNA.

"And please don't say anything to Dad," she pleaded, horrified at the mere thought of her father finding out.

"Dad seems kind of…"

"What?" Chiara asked at the hesitation, panic sprouting in her core.

"He's fine," Marco reassured. "Just seems distracted for some reason."

She allowed herself the moment of relief. "Please don't say anything to him. I'll explain to you as soon as I can," she repeated, willing him to understand.

"The sooner the better."

Chiara released the breath she'd been holding and thanked him profusely before hanging up. At least she'd bought herself some time. But she was much too frazzled now to continue sitting around in a lounge any longer. The unexpected conversation with Marco had taken up the last reserves of her emotional strength.

Time to head back upstairs. There was nothing for it. Maybe she'd catch a break and Evan would be locked away working in the suite office. If so, he might not even notice her coming back in.

* * *

No such luck.

Evan was exactly where she'd left him. He gave her a questioning look when she walked in and shut the door behind her.

"I was too late, it turns out. Didn't get down there in time. The tour must have left a little early."

He merely lifted an eyebrow at her explanation, seemingly convinced. "That's too bad."

She was getting really good at this fibbing thing. She'd have to make several trips to the confessional and shore up some volunteer days at the local shelter as soon as she got back to the States to try to rebalance her karma scales. "I'll try again tomorrow."

"What were you doing all this time?"

Drinking too much tea and trying to convince my brother not to fly across the world in his concern that I might elope with some stranger.

"Just looking into other options as to how to spend my day." That part was true enough. "Nothing came to mind," she added, heading toward the other room to wallow in her boredom.

Evan touched her arm as she walked by him, stopping her in her tracks. Her gaze fell to where he touched her. He had barely lifted a finger in her direction since that night in the hut at the wedding. Neither of them had so much as mentioned it aside from an awkward conversation the next morning about how they'd both gotten carried away by the romantic mood of the wedding. Chiara braced herself against the onslaught of desire that ran through her veins at the mere feel of his hand on her skin.

"Yes?" she asked, eager to move away before she did something to embarrass herself. Like step farther into his arms and ask him to kiss her again, the way she so desperately wanted to.

Evan dropped his hand to his side. "It just so happens I was more productive than I'd hoped to be this morning."

Well, that seemed hard to believe. He was still sitting right where she'd left him this morning. Seemed they both might be doing some fibbing. Then it dawned on her what he might be implying. Was he possibly saying he had some free time?

"What does that mean?" Chiara asked, not daring to hope.

He executed a mini bow that made her laugh. "If you would allow me, I'd be honored to play tour guide for the rest of the day."

Try as she might, Chiara couldn't help the squeal of delight that escaped her. "Really?"

He nodded with a smile that warmed her soul. "Really. It'll be fun. Let me just make a couple calls, then we can be on our way."

"Then go make those calls," she urged, giving him a weak shove before he could change his mind.

The smile on Chiara's face as they made their way out of the lobby to a waiting limo made the lie worthwhile. The truth was he hadn't gotten much done at all after she'd left. His usually laser sharp focus had completely abandoned him. It was hard to drown out the annoying voice. The one in his head that had nagged at him all morning. Telling him he'd been a fool to let Chiara leave without him. When she reappeared, it began to scream that he couldn't waste the second chance he'd been presented with.

She paused and turned to him halfway to the vehicle. "Is that for us?" she asked, pointing to the car.

"That would be why the driver is holding the door open as we approach."

She blinked up at him. "Got it. We're taking a limo to the Great Wall."

"It's over an hour's drive from here. May as well be comfortable."

Still, she didn't move. "You didn't have to do all this, Evan. I would have been happy to take a bus or something. Just as long as you…" But she didn't finish her sentence.

Evan was tempted to press, ask her exactly

what she was about to say. But now the driver was staring at them in confusion.

"Come on." He gently nudged her with a hand at her waist. "It's not a big deal. This is how I usually travel long distances in Beijing."

With clear reluctance, she finally moved, and he helped her into the back, then sat on the opposite bench. The driver reappeared with a steaming pot of tea and a bamboo basket and placed the items on the table between them before settling into the driver's seat.

"Early lunch," he told her and lifted the lid of the basket to reveal several dumplings. He handed her a set of wooden chopsticks.

"No tea for me, thanks," Chiara said, taking the chopsticks and plucking up one of the dumplings.

"You sure? You'll appreciate the warm-up once we get there. This is the coldest time of year to visit the Great Wall."

She nodded. "I'm sure. I had my fill earlier in the lounge of the hotel." She licked her lips after a bite of food and Evan lost his focus for a moment. Her next words brought him back to the present. "I have a confession," she began.

Interesting. And curious. "Oh?"

She set down her chopsticks and leveled her eyes on his. "I didn't really miss the tour group earlier."

"What happened?"

"The truth is I didn't want to go by myself. Or with a group of strangers."

Now he really felt like a heel. He should have just asked her to go with him from the get-go. Such a mistake on his part. What she said next didn't make him feel any better.

"So I feel a little guilty that you went through all this trouble," she said, waving her hands around the car. "Arranging for a limo. One that serves lunch."

Evan leaned toward her over the table. "If we're confessing, I have to come clean about something, too."

"What's that?"

"I lied to you about how much work I got done this morning. In fact, I barely accomplished anything after you left."

She chuckled at his admission. "Why would you lie about that?"

"To give me an excuse to spend the day with you."

CHAPTER TWELVE

HER MOTHER'S CHAPTER books had not prepared her for the view before her. Nor had all the websites and travel guides she'd browsed over the years. Chiara let Evan guide her down the stone pathway, stopping every few feet just to take in the scenery. She couldn't blame the photographers. There was no earthly way to capture the majesty and grandeur that was the Great Wall of China. Godlike mountains as far as her eyes could see, now dusted with a layer of snow just thin enough to have the greenery below peak through. A blue-gray sky framed the horizon. Thick puffy clouds roamed the sky like grand ships

It was also very cold. Skin-numbing, bone-numbing cold. Despite her thick coat and clothing, Chiara felt the chill clear to her center.

Evan must have noticed her shivering. "Too bad we're not here during a summer month," he said. "The weather is much more pleasant for one. And you might have witnessed a traditional Chinese wedding."

"Couples get married here?"

He nodded. "Just not in December."

Another chill ran through her. "I don't blame them." But what a stunning and unforgettable location for a wedding. To be surrounded by this view as you commit yourself to the love of your life. Chiara could just imagine how sacred and beautiful a ceremony held here would be. "What a wonderful way for a couple to begin their life together."

"The only wedding venue visible from space."

They walked toward the closest tower. She could only guess what the view might look like from that height. In her haste, she clumsily stepped on a patch of slick snow and her foot slipped out from beneath her. She braced herself for the inevitable impact of hard stone against her knee and prayed fervently to be spared a broken bone. A miracle spared her just before the tumble, though, as a set of sturdy arms suddenly wrapped around her waist.

Not a miracle but Evan.

"Whoa, steady there." She straightened to thank him. But the words caught in her throat. His face was a mere inch or so from his. The fog of their breath intermingled between them. His now-familiar scent, masculine and woodsy, tickled her nose and sent longing surging through her core. As if in slow motion, he tilted his head closer. The world simply stopped.

Kiss me. Please.

She wanted so badly to say the words aloud. Or to just do it herself, spare him from making the decision by simply reaching for him. Settling her mouth over his and tasting him.

The sound of footsteps nearing them barely registered in her ears. But Evan suddenly straightened and balanced her back on her feet. Then he let her go. A family of three stepped around them with polite smiles. The loss of his nearness had her shaking where she stood. It had nothing to do with the cold this time. The moment was lost, disintegrated like smoke as if it had never happened.

"Let's get to that tower," he said, guiding her gently by the elbow.

The air got cooler and cooler as they climbed up the stone steps. Chiara could hardly bother to notice when they reached the top, however. She felt like she could be flying, like the crow from the book her mother read to her all those years ago.

The view from up here was even more breathtaking. Spiritual even. "I've never felt such a connection to the planet." She hadn't even meant to say it out loud.

The look that passed over Evan's face gave her pause. "You must think I'm being silly," she said with a soft chuckle. "Waxing poetic."

He shook his head in a slow, steady motion. "Actually, I was thinking that was pretty much the exact thought I had the first time I climbed up one of these towers."

"Really?"

"Really."

"How old were you?"

"About ten. My ahma brought me here to visit."

"Your ahma?"

His lips tightened. "She's like a nanny. Or caregiver to a child."

"The one you said was the only person to ever stand up for you as a child."

He swallowed and turned away but not before she saw his features wash over with tenderness. "That's right. She brought me to the Wall for the very first time. Once when it was just this cold. If not colder."

So, not his parents, then. Chiara got the feeling Evan didn't have many memories that involved his parents. Just how distant and cold had they been to their son? If the confrontation with his mother at the wedding was any clue, he hadn't grown up in the warmest environment.

She was trying to figure out a way to ask him that very thing when a cold gust of wind gushed through the tower, her teeth actually chattered hard enough to be heard. She could stay up here simply taking in the scene all day, even longer. But her body was beginning to protest the elements.

Evan unbuttoned his topcoat and unwrapped the scarf from around his neck. He held it out to her. Chiara immediately protested with a shake of her head. The man wasn't even wearing a hat, for heaven's sake. She wasn't about to take his scarf.

He didn't wait for permission, instead draping the scarf around her shoulders and tucking it under her chin.

"Thank you. But how are you not even cold?"

"I've come up here in the winter before. It's not new for me."

The scarf had to be cashmere, soft as air yet rugged enough to protect her from the cold. The description reminded her of the man she was with. Wearing the scarf resurfaced vivid memories of the night they'd spent together back in Singapore. The passion that had combusted between them, her body's heady and strong reaction. And the way she'd felt afterward, encased in his arms, surrounded by the smell of him. His warmth seeping through her skin.

Heaven help her, she wanted badly for it to all happen again.

* * *

Chiara's cheeks were the color of a Bengal rose by the time they made it back to the limo. Evan wanted nothing more than to gather her in his arms in the back seat. Then he'd take her lips with his own and kiss her until she was so far from cold she was burning for him.

Instead, he reached for the pot of steaming hot tea the driver had ready for them and poured her a generous cup. "This will warm you up in no time," he assured, still wishing badly he could do it himself.

Then he could ask the driver to rush them back to the hotel and join her in one of those steamy showers she enjoyed so much. Apparently, the cold hadn't done much to tamper his libido at all.

He recalled the way she'd fallen against him on the way to the watchtower. If that family hadn't walked past them, she would probably be in his arms right now with the divider to the front seat raised for privacy.

Studying her now as she slowly sipped her tea, he vividly remembered the way she'd tasted the last time he'd kissed her. He really shouldn't be heading down that path.

Evan turned his head from her sparkling eyes and rose-red cheeks to stare out the window. This thing with Chiara was never supposed to become a distraction. The only reason she was here was to help him land a business deal.

How had things gotten so complicated between the two of them?

Maybe heading back to the hotel right now wasn't the wisest move. Not if he wanted to try to keep his hands off her. And he absolutely had to keep his hands off her. He had two important meetings coming up that he had to focus on. The tension between them here and now was practically tangible. He knew exactly where it would lead as soon as they were alone together back at the hotel suite.

He cleared his throat before turning back to her. "If you think you're warm enough now to handle another outdoor activity, there is one more stop I'd like to show you."

She narrowed her eyes at him. If he didn't know better, he'd say Chiara had guessed exactly where his thoughts had just traveled and why he was suggesting a detour. "What kind of stop?"

"You mentioned ice skating at Rockefeller Center back in New York."

"You want to go ice skating? Now?"

He nodded once. "Something like that."

About a half hour ride later, Chiara found herself standing in front of a stadium unlike any she'd encountered in the States. Or anywhere else she'd visited for that matter. The place was colossal. With steel lattice beams around the entire structure.

She uttered the only word that came to mind as they approached one of the many entrances. "Wow."

"It's called the Bird's Nest and it was built for the Olympics," Evan explained. "But now it's used for all sorts of activities. And in the winter months, the entire place hosts the Ice and Snow Festival."

Festival was hardly an apt word to describe what they walked into once they entered the building. Massive ice sculptures depicting various cartoons she remembered from her childhood. Brightly decorated Christmas trees. Evan led her through the crowds and into what could only be described as an actual life-sized city sculpted entirely out of ice, complete with a castle and forts surrounded by a circular wall. Chiara felt as if she might have walked into some medieval frozen planet.

"And here I thought we would just be skating."

He winked at her. "Oh, we're going to do that, too. Only, it's not the kind of ice skating you're thinking of."

What other type of skating was there on ice? Chiara got her answer a few minutes later.

Ice cycling. That's what Evan had meant. Chiara Pearson, who thought she'd heard and seen everything as a life-long resident of New York City, who'd been backpacking across the globe for the last seven years, was about to try a sport she hadn't even known existed an hour ago.

It certainly seemed popular. The rink was crowded with all manner of skaters. From small children to elderly grandparents and everything in between. Everyone seemed to be having a grand time. Laughter echoed from every direction.

Once they were on the ice, Evan hopped on the main seat and had her sit behind him. The bike was small. Try as she might to maintain even a sliver of distance, it was no use. Chiara's upper thighs cradled Evan's hips, snug and tight. She had to squeeze her eyes shut and try to ignore the heady sensations rushing through her at the intimate contact.

"You nice and secure back there?" he asked over his shoulder.

If he only knew. "Ready to go," she answered.

He took off before she'd barely gotten the last word out. They moved so fast she had to wrap her arms around Evan's waist for fear of toppling off her seat. How he maneuvered the bike through the crowded rink at such a high speed had to be some sort of learned skill. Or maybe

Evan was the type of man who just happened to be good at everything he did.

Oh, dear. That certainly sounded like she'd become rather keen on him.

Stop overanalyzing.

She made herself focus on Evan's joyous laugh instead. He was thoroughly enjoying himself. Chiara found herself chuckling at the mere joy radiating from Evan as he accelerated and turned on a sharp angle. They came to a stop when he reached the edge of the ice. A teenage couple pulled up alongside them and both gave a friendly smile. The boy motioned with his hands at Evan.

"They're challenging us to a race," he told her. "You up for it?"

A race? With all these other skaters in the way? It seemed rather hazardous. Evan took her pause as an affirmative answer.

A moment later, they were shooting across the ice, skirting around other bikes and skaters. There were so many close calls Chiara squeezed her eyes shut and awaited the inevitable impact more than once. Somehow, Evan avoided colliding with anyone else. He had fast reflexes and animal-like agility. Still, the close encounters were enough to send adrenaline pumping through her body. Or maybe that was due to Evan's proximity. When they finally came to a stop at the opposite end of the rink, Chiara was sure her heart was galloping at the speed of stampeding horses. They'd won the so-called race by several seconds. But the teenagers were smiling good-naturedly when they reached their side. They both gave Evan a small respectful bow, then turned around and rode off.

"That was impressive," she told him.

"Want to try?"

"Sure, why not?" She'd ridden bikes before; how different could it be to ride one on the ice?

But when they reversed positions, this time it was Evan's strong, muscular legs around her hips. His chin sitting on her right shoulder. His breath felt warm on her cheek. His arms wrapped around her waist. Chiara had to remind herself to breath.

Slowly, she began to move the bike forward, their pace much slower than when Evan had had command of the vehicle. She was certain Evan must have been bored out of his mind given how much slower she was going. But he leaned and spoke into her ear. "Take your time. You're doing great."

Silly as it was, she felt a surge of pleasure at his compliment. When had it become so important to her that Evan be pleased with her? In fact, her feelings for him were growing more complicated by the minute. And darned if she knew what to do about it.

It took several minutes, but they finally reached the entrance after doing a half circle around the rink. Evan assisted her off the bike. "Well done, Ms. Pearson."

She performed a mini bow. "Thank you. Though I won't be winning any impromptu ice bike races any time soon as you did."

"Still, I'd say you deserve a warm drink."

Within minutes, Evan had turned the bike in and they were seated at a wooden bench with steaming cups of coconut milk and a plate of delicate biscuits. Chiara watched the skaters on the ice, taking note of one small girl who repeatedly slipped and fell, stubbornly refusing help from her mom and giggling with each topple. The image brought forth a storm of memories from her own childhood of all the times her mother had taken her skating at Rockefeller Center. She'd been just as stubborn. Her mother had been patient as a saint with her.

"What has you smiling so fondly?" Evan asked.

She took a sip of her drink before answering. "Just remembering all the times my mother took me skating at Rockefeller Center as a child."

"Explains why you're such a natural on the ice."

She had to chuckle at that. "Trust me, those first few times I remember spending more time on my bottom than upright on the skates. My mom would just patiently wait for me to get up because I refused any help."

"Sounds like she was very indulgent with you."

"My dad would certainly say she was. Too much so." She sighed with deep sadness. "I wish you could have met her." Whoa. Where had that come from? But now that the words were out, Chiara realized just how true they were.

Her mother would have been beyond impressed with Evan Kim, had she known him. He was exactly the type of man Mama would have been proud of if she'd had another son. Or son-in-law. Chiara gave her head a shake. Another wayward thought she had no business thinking.

Evan surprised her with his next words when he responded. "I wish it, too, Chiara," he said, then took her hand in his.

Hours later, after they'd left the dinner meeting and made it back to their hotel suite, Evan was still thinking about the admission he'd made to Chiara. He should have never told her he would have liked to meet her mother. It was personal, implied a personal intimacy he had no business acknowledging out loud.

Chiara turned to him with a bright smile, unpinning her hair and shaking it loose. "That went well, didn't it?"

He nodded. "We played our parts perfectly. Everyone there is convinced we're a legitimate couple."

She took two hesitant steps toward him. Evan kept his feet firmly planted where he stood. He knew what was to come next. They'd been heading to this conclusion all night. But the next move had to be hers. The decision had to be hers and hers alone. "I didn't have to do much pretending, Evan."

Seemed it was the day for honest admissions. She took another shaky breath before she spoke again. "And I'd like very much to stop pretending tonight."

Evan did the only thing he could think to do. Spreading his arms wide, he beckoned her to him. Chiara reached him within seconds, tight against his length. Then his lips found hers.

No more words needed to be spoken. They both knew what the other wanted. There'd be no denying. Somehow, when he wasn't looking or paying attention, he'd begun to care for her in a way that felt utterly new and foreign. He wasn't sure what that meant for him. But there'd be time to examine all that later. Right now, she was here.

Silently, gently, he broke the kiss and led her by the hand to the bedroom. A nagging voice whispering in his head told him that he needed to examine this, whatever was happening between them. Too many lines were being blurred, too many boundaries crossed. But in this moment, Evan knew couldn't take his next breath if he made himself turn away from her. Later, he would have to come to terms with what it all meant for him. With what Chiara might mean to him. But not now. Now there was only the two of them. They had all night together.

It was near dawn when he felt her awaken in his arms, rousing him as well.

"Ready to do some skiing in a couple days? By this time tomorrow we'll be in Switzerland."

"I know. To be seen on the slopes as the happy couple."

"That's right. St. Moritz is a magnet for celebrities, so it always draws a lot of international paparazzi. I figure we'll stop there first and spend a few days skiing and enjoying the mountain air. It will give us one last chance to be seen and maybe photographed together before the final meeting with the Italian AI executives."

"Got it." She executed a mini stretch, never leaving his arms. "I hope I don't embarrass you with my skills. It's been ages since I've been on the slopes."

"I'm sure it's a lot like riding a bike. Once you learn, you don't forget."

"Hmm. I hope so." A chuckle escaped her lips. "I'll have you know that once, at the immature age of seven, I went skiing in a full pirate's outfit over my ski suit. Complete with plastic sword and patterned bandanna under my helmet."

Evan had to laugh at the image.

"You did?"

She nodded against his bare chest. "Yep. I decided I was going to be the only skiing pirate on the slopes that day and my mother obliged. Went to the costume store and found me everything I needed to become a bandit of the seas. To wear in the snowy mountains."

"You must have made quite the picture."

"Marco thought so. He was both amused and horrified to be seen with his swashbuckling sister. My dad just shook his head."

She turned to face him, bracing her forearms on his chest as she spoke. "See, Dad thought Mom was too permissive when I asked to do such things. Said she never told me no. But he always said it with a rather indulgent smile on his face as well," she added, then rested her head on his chest. "It's funny."

"What is?"

"I don't typically talk about my mother this much. It's too painful. But with you, I can't seem to keep my mouth shut about her."

Evan stroked her hair, touched that she could confide in him about the loving parent she'd lost. She said she'd been indulged as a child. He couldn't think of a single time he might have used that word to describe himself. Even his ahma, as affectionate as she was, had been strict about his schedule and his studies.

He and Chiara had drastically different childhoods. In fact, they didn't have very much in common at all. For one, Chiara belonged to a loving and devoted family. She always had.

The way Chiara spoke of her parents and brother was both touching and bittersweet. Despite the devastating loss of her mother, there was nothing but love echoed in her recollection of her childhood whenever she spoke of it. Her voice filled with tenderness in each word.

A faint curl of envy swirled in his chest, then grew to a low ache. He would never have that. The comfort of a loving and devoted family. Hell, if anything ever happened to him, it wouldn't even make a difference in anyone's life. What a devastatingly brutal truth that was. Besides Louis, would anyone even care if he were gone?

Without thought, he dropped a peck of a kiss atop Chiara's head. She shifted in his arms and nestled her back closer against his chest. In about a week or so, she would be out of his life as well. Back home to the loving arms of her father and brother to spend the holidays in a welcoming home she'd grown up in. While he'd be back in Singapore. Or maybe he'd return home to Bali. Alone. Spending Christmas like any other day. A hollowness settled in his chest at the thought.

It was for the best. He did better on his own. The one time he'd grown close to anyone, she'd been tragically taken from him with no other source of comfort to help him deal with the loss. He'd had to mourn her on his own. Evan didn't need that kind of pain again.

Look how successful he was. How far he'd come. He would have never accomplished so much in such a short period of time if there'd been any emotional distractions in his life.

No reason to change what had worked so well for him up until now. Not even for Chiara Pearson.

CHAPTER THIRTEEN

St. Moritz, Switzerland

CHIARA HAD NO idea how it had happened, but somehow the last couple of weeks had flown past in the blink of an eye. In just a few short days, it would be Christmas, and she'd be back in the States to make her pilgrimage to the house in Vermont and finally see her family. And Evan would be on his way somewhere else, back to his old life.

They'd literally and figuratively be going their separate ways. Who knew when she might see him again, if ever?

One day, one moment, at a time. It was the only way she was going to get through this. Staring at the large glass window overlooking the snow-peaked alpine mountains, she heard Evan walk into the room. He was fully dressed in a casual sports jacket and pressed khakis.

"Are you going out?"

He nodded once. "I have a brief lunch meeting with the woman who runs my charity organization."

"Your charity?"

"Yeah. I donate to various causes, mostly children's issues and some refugee organizations. At one point, it just became easier to form a foundation. And put someone else in charge of running it."

Huh. She'd had no idea. As close as they'd become, there was so much about this man she still didn't know. So much he hadn't revealed. He'd founded his own charity. As if there wasn't enough about the man she admired already.

"It just so happens that the president resides in Switzerland. Priya offered to take the train and meet me here to catch up on the latest."

Priya. An image popped into Chiara's mind of a long-legged, statuesque beauty with thick ebony hair and doe-like eyes.

He hadn't thought to invite her to this breakfast meeting. And she had no reason to feel slighted in any way by that. In fact, she was no different than this president he was about to meet with. She was merely an employee, after all.

A nagging curl of doubt nevertheless crept into her brain. So far, Evan had taken her to every meeting and function. Why was this one different? Was it because he was meeting with a woman? Had they shared some kind of intimacy in the past?

She gave her head a brief shake. None of her business. She had no claim to him whatsoever.

He must have read the direction of her thoughts. "Did you want to come along? I just figured you'd want some time to rest up after our long flight and before we hit the slopes later today."

She did. So very much. But for all the wrong reasons. Reasons she had to squelch and bury deep, never to be uncovered again.

She shook her head in response. "No. You're right. I could use some downtime before hitting the slopes."

He reached her in two strides. Took her hand and kissed the inside of her palm. A fairly innocent gesture. Still, it sent a flush of heat rushing through her center and out toward her limbs.

"Good. I want you fresh and rested for that final meeting with the Italians."

"Right." Though how she was supposed to pull off the facade of happy fiancée when all she could think about was how they'd be parting ways so soon afterward, she had no idea. "No pressure."

He dropped her hand. "It's our final shot to

convince them to take a chance and invest in my expansion."

Chiara could only offer a weak smile in response. Here she was, practically woeful at spending the morning without him as he had breakfast with a female associate. While Evan's sole focus remained his business goals and the part Chiara was here to play to help him achieve them. The only reason she was here, really.

That made her all kinds of a fool.

Evan guided Chiara to the bottom of the hill and helped her hop onto the moving gondola car, then quickly joined her in the seat. "No pirate costume this time?"

She smiled at him. "I guess I forgot to pack it."

"Just as well. I would have had to draw the line at the eye patch."

He'd been right about Chiara's ability to ski. It only took a couple of runs down the mountain for her to get her bearings and ski like someone who'd learned as a child.

Costume or not, Chiara looked beyond enticing in the form-fitting ski suit and parka. Even dressed in layers of fleece and down, she posed the sexiest, most fetching picture. Not for the first time that day, he wanted to whisk her off the mountain and rush them back to the hotel where he could proceed to slowly peel all those layers off her and warm her chilled skin.

Stop it. They were only here in the hopes of having one or two snaps of them taken for one final hit on a gossip website. He was in the final stretch, about to grasp all that he'd been reaching for professionally for the past several months.

Yet, all he could think of was holding Chiara in his arms.

He had to snap out of it. Now was not the time to let his hormones run the show. He had to stop thinking about her in such lurid ways. And he absolutely had to keep his distance.

Fate seemed to have a different plan.

They'd reached the top of the ride when a loud grinding noise echoed through the air and their car came to a gradual stop. Great. They were stuck. Evan knew from past experience that it could take some time to get the lifts moving again. The small speaker below the seat came to life to explain that there'd been a minor glitch in need of repair, first in Swiss, then translated to English, followed by several other languages. So much for keeping his distance. How was he to keep his hands off her when they were stuck up here alone for who knew how long?

"Huh," Chiara said next to him, leaning slightly over the edge of the gondola to look down. "We're rather high up." Her words were followed by a full body shiver.

She was either cold or frightened. Or both. He was only human, for heaven's sake. He couldn't very well just let her sit there, shaking. He wrapped his arm around her shoulders and pulled her close against his side.

"It's okay. This happens often here. They'll have us moving in no time," he assured, hoping he wasn't lying to her yet again.

The tension in her shoulders relaxed and she leaned into him, resting her head on his shoulder.

"Try to focus on the view," he advised. "It's beautiful up here." That statement was most definitely not a lie. Snow-capped mountains as far as the eye could see, a bright, light blue sky and tiny snowflakes had begun to fall in the few short seconds they'd been up there.

"All the same, I'd rather be looking at it from the glass wall of the hotel suite," Chiara said. Another shudder racked through her body.

Evan tilted her chin up to his face with one finger. "Hey, it's okay. We'll be moving in no time."

She nodded, her eyes far from convinced. "I've been stuck in a lift before. Just never this high up." Her bottom lip quivered, and the small motion led to Evan's undoing. All thoughts of keeping his distance fled his mind. Instead, he shifted her onto his lap, held her tight. When she reached for his lips with her own, he didn't have the strength to deny her. He took her mouth with his own in a deep lingering kiss. Now, it was his turn to shiver, for entirely different reasons.

He'd been fooling himself to think he could stay away from her. Despite the mounds of clothing between them, Evan felt every inch of her against his body. Her warmth seemed to seep through her clothing straight to his bones. He couldn't get enough of the taste of her. When she moaned against his mouth, he could only kiss her deeper. He wanted to hear her moan for him every day for the rest of his life.

Mercifully, in that moment, their gondola car jerked to life.

Evan made himself pull away, took several deep breaths before he could get his mouth to work. "See, we're moving already."

Shifting in the seat, he moved out from under her until she was no longer in his lap. Dazed, Chiara looked up at him, her eyes confused.

Well, he was pretty confused himself. He'd only meant to comfort her. But it had turned into so much more.

"There's something I've been putting off."

Chiara finally found the nerve to go interrupt Evan at the dining room table of their hotel suite. He'd been working all morning. They were to ski again later that afternoon, but she had a more pressing errand she needed to run.

"What's that?" he asked her absentmindedly in response to her statement, barely glancing up from the laptop screen.

She pulled out the chair next to him, moved it closer to his side and sat down. Perhaps she was being too forward, but surely the man didn't have to work quite so much. It was the holiday season, after all. Most of the world had slowed down their productivity. Surely, Evan could do so as well. "It's not so much that I've been putting it off exactly," she answered him. "But I didn't really have the money. Not until very recently."

"Money for what?"

"I need to do some shopping."

"What kind of shopping? I thought the personal shopper secured everything you needed."

"Not presents."

She watched as he typed some more, then pounded on the backspace button.

"Presents?"

Chiara blew out an exasperated breath. Honestly, for such a brilliant mind, he could be quite clueless at times. "It's Christmas in a few short days, Evan."

Releasing a sigh, he turned away from the laptop at last. Finally, she had his full attention. "And?"

Oh, come now. Was he honestly not seeing the direction she was headed in? "And I'd like to go find some presents. For my father and brother. And a couple of other people back in the States."

"Why didn't you just say so? There's a major shopping center about a mile away. With several top fashion house boutiques. I can call a car for you."

"Don't you have people you want to shop for? What about Louis? Or any of your employees?"

He narrowed his eyes on her. "Of course. My assistant takes care of it for me. She's already done so."

Chiara's exasperation was replaced with a resounding sadness. Christmas for Evan was such a cold and practical experience in his life. "Don't you want to pick anything out yourself to give them? It would make the gift so much more personal."

"Are you asking me to come shopping with you?"

"I think it would do you good," Chiara answered and meant it. "To experience a little Christmas cheer."

Evan practically rolled his eyes at her, an indication of what he felt about that idea. He tapped her playfully on the nose. "I think you just want my company. Admit it."

"I admit it."

The smile he gave her had her blood pressure rising and she had to force her focus back on the conversation at hand.

"Fine. If it's that important to you," Evan said, closing the lid of his laptop.

She nodded once. "It is."

He pulled out his cell phone. "I'll call for a car."

Chiara glanced at the crystal blue sky outside the glass balcony door. The bright rays of the sun kissed the snow-topped mountains. She reached for Evan's hand before he could dial. From what she'd seen of the town so far since arriving, it was decked out and festively decorated for the season. "I think we should walk."

How had he gotten roped into this? Evan couldn't remember the last time he'd gone shopping for anything. He'd always had people who were paid to do it for him.

One glance at Chiara and he had the answer to his question. The smile she wore lit up her entire face. She was practically skipping next to him as they made their way to the shopping plaza. He'd never seen anyone so excited to get things for other people.

"Have you thought any more about what you might get Louis?" she asked.

He had not. "I'm hoping I know it when I see it."

She aimed the full force of that brilliant smile in his direction. "That could work. I've found more than one gift that way."

A few minutes later, they approached the palatial structure that housed some of the most luxe stores in Switzerland. Evan turned toward the entrance but realized Chiara had stopped a few feet behind him. She was focused on several booths set up across the street. A number of craftsmen had set up tables and displays with their various wares. Not unusual for this time of year.

"Can we go there first?" she asked.

He'd barely gotten the words out before she'd already begun to cross the street. He followed her to the first table. It held several trays of blown glass ornaments. "Oh, these are beautiful." She pointed to one shaped as some sort of complicated icicle. "I'll take that one please." The vendor flashed her a smile and began wrapping the item.

"Don't you want one? For your tree?"

"I don't really see one I like." He wasn't going

to tell her that he never even bothered with a tree. Someone like Chiara, who placed such an importance on the holidays, wouldn't be able to understand but Evan never bothered to decorate for Christmas in any way. What was the point?

In fact, he wasn't even sure why he was bothering with this trip other than to humor Chiara. But much to his surprise, within minutes Evan found himself purchasing several boxes of homemade candy at one of the booths for his employees. At yet another, he found a hand-sewn necktie that he purchased for Louis along with a matching scarf for his new wife.

Go figure. He was actually Christmas shopping.

For her part, Chiara was armed with several shopping bags holding gifts, including a hand-knitted wool scarf for her brother that bore the likeness of a goofy cartoon yeti. For her father, she'd picked out a handcrafted leather wallet. Costume jewelry for a couple of girlfriends in New York rounded out her purchases. And somehow, she was carrying another small bag with an item Evan hadn't even seen her purchase. He had no idea what it could be, but he wasn't going to ask. If she'd wanted him to know, she would have told him.

"Are you ready to go into some real stores now?" he asked.

Chiara turned her focus toward the building that had once been a chateau for a Swiss count but had long since been converted to a luxe shopping center. "No, thank you." She lifted her bags. "I have everything I came for."

She really was something else. Most women he knew would have made a beeline for the boutiques. Or the designer handbag store.

Between them, they'd spent a fraction of the figure Evan might have guessed they'd spend. Yet, somehow, Chiara had gotten her family and friends the perfect gifts.

He hadn't done so bad himself.

When Evan had told her they'd be dining on a train, Chiara couldn't have imagined such a glamorous setting. The meal car reminded her of one of the grander ballrooms in the Grandview Hotel. Walls lined with thick velvet, mahogany tables, rich upholstered chairs.

She and Evan were taking the train to Liechtenstein where they would meet with the executives one final time before a decision was made. One of the Italian gentlemen owned a villa in that city and was there for the holidays. They'd been welcomed to spend the night, then travel back to their hotel in St. Moritz in the morning. All in all, a dizzying twenty-four hours. Such was the life of a jet-setter like Evan Kim, she supposed. A life that would definitely take some getting used to. Not that she had to worry about it.

A tuxedoed server handed them two flutes of champagne as they made their way to their reserved table. To think, she'd thought she might be overdressed in her satin burgundy wraparound dress and high-heeled black suede boots. Everyone on board was just as swanky. A lot of jewelry donned the necks and wrists of their fellow travelers. For his part, Evan looked beyond dashing in a dark navy suit that brought out the dark ebony highlights of his hair and a crisp shirt the color of the sky.

Did she even fit in amongst these people?

And how would she do tonight as she faced the final test?

She had to be on her toes, no mistakes or all their efforts these past few weeks would be for naught. Evan would be so disappointed. In her.

Distracted by the stunning view that greeted her, her worries found a back seat as they took their seats at the table and the train began to move. A large window by their table afforded her an unobstructed look at the majestic mountains that surrounded them.

"Quite the scene, huh?" Evan asked, unbuttoning his suit jacket.

"It's magnificent."

"I think beautiful would be a more apt description." But he wasn't looking out the window as he spoke; he was looking directly at her. Her heart did a funny little jump in her chest. Before she could think of any kind of response that didn't have her sounding like a giddy schoolgirl with a crush, a waiter appeared with a sweaty bottle of champagne to refill their glasses. He was immediately followed by another who placed a fondue set on the table between them and lit the bottom burner. A blue flame began to glow beneath the pot. Yet another server then arrived with a tray of cheese squares, crusty bread pieces and a dozen silver skewers. With a friendly smile, she dropped the cheese into the pot and poured some kind of alcohol out of a tall glass bottle, then stirred the contents.

"Enjoy," she told them with a slight accent, when the concoction had reached the consistency of thick, rich cheesy sauce.

Chiara had no doubt that she would. The smell of the melting cheese had her mouth watering. Following Evan's lead, she stabbed one of the bread pieces with a skewer and dipped it into the cheese. The gooey warm flavor exploded on her tongue when she began to eat.

"This is unlike any cheese fondue I've ever had," she told him, helping herself to another piece.

"I'm glad you like it."

Several minutes passed and she allowed herself to indulge. But Evan seemed to have slowed. He'd barely eaten more than a few bites. "Do you? Like it?" she asked.

He blinked at her. She pointed to the fondue. "Oh. Yeah. It's delicious," he finally replied after several beats. "I guess I'm just not that hungry today."

Either that or he was distracted. She reached across the table and took his hand, gave it a gentle squeeze of reassurance. "Evan, tonight will go great. You know they're impressed with your accomplishments. And we'll be proving to them that you're a stable, reliable businessman who's ready to settle down and get married." Her words held an inflection of confidence she didn't really feel. In fact, Evan's nervousness was only serving to heighten hers.

He placed his free hand on top of hers, sandwiching her small fingers between his own. "You're right. Of course."

She gave him a bright smile. "Of course I am. Now, eat some cheese. Or I'll be the only one having it and will arrive at this gentleman's house bloated and much too full."

The afternoon gradually started to grow darker as Chiara watched the view outside turn from one majestic scene to another. They reached an arched bridge that towered over the ravine below and she could swear they were suspended in midair and flying between the mountains.

Just when she thought she couldn't eat another bite, the cheese fondue set was removed to be replaced with another one, this time filled with chunks of chocolate. Again, a bottom burner was lit and the delicacy slowly began to melt. Another tray then appeared, piled high with colorful fruit—berries, melons, kiwi and bright citrus. Chiara picked the plumpest strawberry she could find and skewered it, then dipped it into the rich, creamy chocolate sauce. The combination of ripe fruit and sweet candy tasted like a treat from the gods.

Heaven help her, she couldn't escape the moan of pleasure that escaped her lips.

She looked up to find Evan staring at her, a blend of amusement and…yes, desire showing clearly in his eyes. Without thinking, she skewered another piece of fruit, dipped it, then reached it over. Evan leaned in and took the offering, chewing slowly, his eyes never leaving hers.

It all came crashing down on her, then. There was no denying. As she sat here, hand-feeding Evan Kim dessert in a speeding train car across the Swiss mountains, Chiara had to admit what she'd been brushing away for several days now.

She was wholly, desperately and undoubtedly head over heels in love with the man.

CHAPTER FOURTEEN

THE MEETING SEEMED to be going really well. Everything Chiara translated so far sounded positive for Evan. Almost as if the deal were already done and they were just discussing the specifics. By the time they walked out of the chalet tomorrow morning, Chiara had no doubt Evan's deal would be signed and sealed.

They'd done it!

She could finally relax some of the tension that had gripped her since this morning and start to breathe a bit easier. About this meeting, anyway. As for the rest, she had no idea what she was going to do. How would he react if she just told him how she felt about him? What would he say if she were to admit that she was in no way ready to say goodbye?

He had to see what was so obvious—they couldn't just walk away from this after all that had happened, not after everything they'd shared. What they'd come to mean to each other.

Chiara puffed out a deep breath, watching as the men began with the paperwork.

But what exactly did Chiara and Evan mean to each other? She couldn't define it. All she was certain of was that she wasn't ready to turn her back on it.

But she had no idea if Evan felt at all the same way. She was still working up the courage and thinking of a way to ask him when they were led to the suite in the chalet they'd be spending the night in. A celebratory bottle of chilled Chasselas sat waiting for them on the center coffee table. With deft motions, Evan uncorked the bottle and poured into the two goblets by the bottle. He handed one to her.

"Thank you."

He took a sip of his wine. "No, thank you. You're the reason I've gotten this deal. It would have never worked without you by my side."

Chiara tried not to let the swell of disappointment at his words crush her too deeply. Of course, he was excited about his business expansion. She could give him that. It didn't mean that was the only reason he was happy to have her by her side at the moment.

He walked over to the balcony doors and pulled them wide open, then stepped out onto the concrete. Turning, he held his glass up in a salute to her, his smile as bright as the crescent moon above. If only she could return that smile with one of her own. If only she could pretend she wasn't falling apart inside, that he still hadn't said anything about a change in plans.

She had to get some answers. She had to know. About where he stood. How he felt now that their official mission was accomplished. With heavy feet, Chiara walked over to meet him outside.

The first thing he said to her gave her a slight clue, and it wasn't encouraging in the least. "I'll wire the funds to your account tonight. You've more than earned every penny. And your plane ticket back to New York is on me. Consider it a bonus."

Earned. Bonus. Evan was all business. While inside, her heart was shattering in her chest.

Now or never. She had to take the chance. Without giving herself the opportunity to second-guess, she blurted out the question that had been haunting her for several days now. "Would you want to come with me? To New York. Then to my family's place in Vermont?"

He lowered his glass, his smile fading. He cleared his throat before he spoke. "Chiara, I can't. Thank you for the invitation. But I just can't."

Every last shred of hope she'd been harboring disintegrated into confetti. He wasn't even going to pretend to take her up on her offer. "It's not that you can't. It's that you don't want to. Why Evan?"

He thrust his free hand into his pants pocket, tilted his head. "It's not that simple of an answer."

"It is from where I'm standing. Please, tell me why you would rather spend the holidays alone in your penthouse in Bali rather than spend that time with me."

"Chiara, it's not fair of you to ask me such things. That was never part of the deal."

She lifted her chin, ignoring the arrow of pain he'd just pierced her heart with. "I know that's how things started with us. But you can't tell me things aren't different now."

At his silence, she pressed on. "Evan, I don't know how to explain the feelings I've developed for you." Yep, she was definitely all in now. No turning back. "Except to say that I feel as if I've known you my whole life. Like we met eons ago and just lost touch for some reason."

His shoulders lifted in a mini shrug. "I'm flattered, Chiara. Really. Thank you."

That was it? His response to what she'd admitted was to thank her? This couldn't be happening.

"It's so easy for you to abandon people, isn't it? You walked away from your parents never to look back, after all." If the stricken expression on Evan's face was anything to go by, she had gone too far. But it was too late to turn back now. "If you'll take some unsolicited advice, I think you should try to reconcile with them. You never know when it might be too late."

His eyes narrowed on her face. "Advice, is it? Because you lost your mom."

She could only nod.

He tossed the contents of his goblet over the railing. "That's not advice. And it isn't about you," he said without a trace of kindness in his voice. "You can't compare what you lost with something I never had."

A gust of wind blew through the air and brought goose bumps to the surface of her skin. Even now, in her utter hurt and humiliation, a part of her wanted Evan to step over to her and warm her up in his arms. He took a step in her direction and a surge of hope shot through her. But it was short-lived as he brushed past her instead to walk back inside.

Chiara sucked in a much-needed breath and turned to join him. He was shrugging out of his suit jacket and grabbing his toiletries when she stepped inside the bedroom. The set of his shoulders told her everything she needed to know. The conversation was over. So much had been said between them, yet so much left unsaid. And it appeared it would stay that way.

"We should get some sleep," he told her. "We have a long day of travel in front of us tomorrow."

Chiara swallowed past the lump of pain that had settled like a brick at the base of her throat. They'd be traveling in entirely different directions. Wordlessly, she made her way to the bathroom.

When she emerged from the shower, Evan had already settled himself on the sofa and appeared to be asleep. So that was it, then. No more discussion. He'd made it very clear what he wanted. And that was to have nothing more to do with her. She grabbed the thick afghan draped over the loveseat and softly covered him with it. Evan didn't so much as stir.

Chiara crawled under the covers, too tired and broken to argue with him about sleeping on an uncomfortable couch.

She spent most of the night willing the tears not to fall.

Who knew he had such convincing thespian skills? Or strength of will for that matter. It had taken all he had not to take hold of Chiara's wrists and pull her down with him on the sofa when she'd draped the afghan over him. Instead, he'd somehow managed to keep his eyes shut, feigning sleep.

He should have seen this coming. He should have known Chiara wasn't the kind of woman who could surrender her heart and then just walk away. Part of him had known, he had to admit. He just hadn't wanted to face it until he had to.

He had meant to talk to her, had every intention of telling her on the drive back to St. Moritz tomorrow morning that, although he would cherish what they'd shared these past few weeks, he was in no position to entertain anything long-term. It just wasn't in his DNA to commit to someone. Anyone.

The only time he'd felt close to another human being the end result had been tragic and sudden, leaving him scarred. With no one to turn to, to help him process or grieve.

But he hadn't had the chance to tell Chiara any of that. She'd taken him by surprise with her invitation. Now, it was too late to tell her much of anything.

He listened to her soft, steady breathing just a few feet away. He would wager she wasn't sleeping, either. What a sorry state of affairs. If only they could do the whole night over. Not that anything fundamental would change. They'd still be going their separate ways. But he might have been able to spare her some of the hurt and pain that had been so clear in her eyes.

He might have explained it all better. Explained how he had no business intruding on her family unit. Pretending to be part of something he could never be part of. During Christmas of all times.

He might have tried harder to help her better understand. Maybe he'd try first thing tomorrow morning to tell her the honest truth. That he never went where he didn't belong.

Chiara was gone when he awoke the next morning, the bed empty and meticulously made. Evan wasn't sure when or how, but somehow he'd managed to fall asleep before the light of dawn and hadn't even heard her leave.

He was about to run out and search the main house when he eyed the engagement ring and a piece of ivory paper sitting atop the duvet in the center of the bed. It served to confirm what he already knew in his soul. She was gone.

With heavy feet, he walked over to read the note.

Evan,
Forgive me. But I couldn't bear the thought of traveling back together after last night. I've taken what I had with me and have de-

cided to go straight to the airport to make my way back home. I've told the housing staff to thank our hosts on my behalf and explain that I was eager to start my day while you prefer to sleep in. Please forward my belongings to the Grand York Hotel in New York. Only my belongings. Nothing more.

The next few words were written in a much shakier hand, as if she were uncertain she wanted to print the words.

I will cherish every moment of the past few weeks and wish you all the success you hope to achieve. Love, C.

Evan reread every word, unblinking until the letters began to swim before his eyes. He'd really made a mess of things. Chiara was gone.

Biting out a curse, he crumpled the paper in his fist and slammed the wall hard enough to disturb an oil painting of the Alps hanging inches above. He caught it before it could fall and haphazardly rehung it, not caring that it now hung askew.

His gaze fell back to the bed. He'd been so focused on the ring and the note that he'd almost missed it—a rectangular white cardboard box with a red satin ribbon sat in the center of the pillow. His name was scrawled in calligraphy on the lid. With shaky fingers, he unwrapped the ribbon and lifted the top. Inside the box sat a wooden sculpture whittled in the shape of a Christmas tree. A tag attached to the stump read *a tree of your own.*

Evan's breath caught as he handled the small work of art. Chiara must have gotten this for him the day they'd gone Christmas shopping, when he hadn't been paying attention.

So she'd seen right through his lie about not buying one of the glass ornaments because he didn't like them. Why was he surprised? In just a few short weeks, Chiara Pearson had somehow come to know him better than anyone else he could name. She'd also grown to care deeply about him. And he'd thrown that back in her face when she'd told him so.

His phone vibrated in his pocket. A surge of hope shot through his chest.

Chiara.

But it wasn't her who appeared on his phone screen when he fished the device out.

"Hey, man, why are you calling me? You're supposed to be on your honeymoon." Evan knew he sounded overly curt. Right this moment, he didn't much care.

Louis's response was a hearty chuckle. "Had

to. After seeing you and your lovely fiancée's pictures all over my tablet on your ski trip in Switzerland. How's the wedding planning going, anyway?"

Evan just couldn't do it; he didn't have it in him to lie anymore. Not to his best friend. Before he knew what he intended, he blurted out the whole convoluted story, ending with the fact that his temporary fiancée hadn't even wanted to say goodbye to him before leaving at the crack of dawn.

A long pause followed his diatribe. Evan heard nothing but his friend's shallow breaths as he took it all in. "So, you're saying none of it was real?"

Evan swallowed back the bile that had gathered at the back of his throat. "That's right. I'm sorry I lied to you, man. I would have come clean sooner, but you had other things going on."

"No apology needed," Louis said without any hesitation. "It's just funny."

"What is?"

"It all looked pretty real to me."

Huh. Evan wasn't sure how to respond to that. His friend didn't give him a chance to try to come up with a way as he continued, "Evan, you're a fool if you don't try to figure out just how real it was."

* * *

Maybe she'd been impulsive, leaving the chalet. But Chiara knew it would have destroyed her to have to spend one more minute with Evan, knowing he cared less for her than she did for him.

If he even cared for her at all.

How could she have read him so wrong? All those times he'd touched her, caressed her, loved her—none of it had meant anything to him. Maybe he just figured it was an added benefit of the bargain they'd struck up that first day. She'd certainly been a willing participant. Evan had never once suggested there was anything emotionally relevant between them. She'd gone ahead and given her heart, anyway.

Her hired car pulled up to the departure area of Lugano Airport and she dabbed at her eyes before exiting. Tossing her two bags over her shoulder, she made her way to the entrance.

Her solo backpacking adventure had come to an end. She didn't know yet what was in store for her back in the States, but her jaunts to various exotic cities abroad were over. She could only hope she'd done her mom proud by visiting enough of the locations Gabriella Pearson would have loved to see herself.

The terminal was bright and cheery, decorated with wreaths and festive, colorful ribbons.

Artificial Christmas trees lit up every corner. A Swiss version of "The First Noel" blared through a network of speakers that followed her as she walked to the ticket gate. The Swiss certainly knew how to decorate for Christmas. The airport was almost as festively geared up as their hotel had been. It was also very, very crowded. Perhaps hopping in a taxi and bee-lining to the airport before so much as buying a ticket wasn't the wisest thing she might have done. But she had her passport and a debit card, which now actually had sufficient funds behind it. What more did she need to make it back home?

But when Chiara reached the gate, the answer to that question wasn't a terribly welcome one. A ticker flashing across every screen announced that all flights back to La Guardia were canceled. Apparently, a major snowstorm was wreaking havoc on half the hemisphere.

The tears she'd somehow managed to hold back all this time were finally unstoppable. This was it. She had nowhere to go. After all she'd been through, all the silly endeavors and playing at being engaged just to get the money to travel back, she wasn't going to make it back home, after all.

All of it had been for naught.

Here she was. Stuck in an airport, unable to

go back to the hotel to face Evan. And unable to board a plane that would have taken her to the loving embrace of her family.

With shaky fingers and her eyes blurry from tears, she pulled her phone out of her pocket to deliver the bad news to her father. It immediately slipped out of her hand and fell to the floor. Chiara could only watch helplessly as the screen cracked down the center. Great. Now she would have to replace her phone, too. Though relieved to find it still appeared functional, Chiara couldn't bring herself to call her father. She just couldn't do it. Not yet. Papa would understand—there wasn't much she could do about the weather and he knew that—but he was going to be, oh, so disappointed. She'd promised him she'd be there for Christmas, after three long years of spending the holidays apart.

She needed air. Suddenly, the cheery and festive decorations and the blaring Christmas carol only served to mock her predicament. Alone in an airport three days before Christmas.

Clutching her cracked phone to her chest and wiping away yet another tear with her sleeve, Chiara ran out the doors as fast as her legs could carry her, barely waiting for the sliding glass doors to fully open.

Finding an empty bench by the road, she dropped her bag and purse onto the ground and sat, slumping into the cold wood. She had to pull herself together. She was safe, in a public place, and as soon as the snow cleared, she would begin to make her way home finally. The delayed flight was just a minor glitch.

So why did she feel like sobbing?

As much as she wanted to talk to someone, she didn't have the heart to call her father or brother just yet to announce that she was going to be at least a day late. Another familiar choice came to mind. Quickly calculating the time difference, she pulled up the contact she had in mind. Nuri would have just finished her shift and arrived back home. Her friend picked up on the first ring.

"Hey, *teman*. Nice to hear from you. Been seeing you in some of the society sites. I want to hear all about it."

If she only knew. When Chiara didn't answer right away, her friend immediately picked up that something was wrong. "Are you all right? Where are you, Chiara?"

"I'm fine. Really. It's just, I needed to hear a friendly voice."

"Tell me. All of it."

Where to begin. Chiara filled in as much of the story as she could without succumbing to more tears. When she was done, she heard Nuri's gasp of astonishment. "All that matters is that you're all right."

Chiara hadn't even realized how much she'd missed the other woman until hearing her voice. That thought just sent another wave of sadness rushing through her chest. She should have stayed in Bali and found another way to earn the money home. That way at least her heart would still be intact.

"But, Chiara, do you mean to tell me that you just left? The very next morning after your argument?"

Chiara sniffled and wiped away another tear. "I'd say it qualified as more than a minor argument, Nuri."

"Maybe so. But I don't recall you being the type to run. From anything. Why did you do so this time?"

The words pounded through Chiara's head. Did Nuri have a point? Instead of seeing things through with Evan, had she taken the easy way out by running off with her tail between her legs? After giving her friend a half-hearted non-answer, Chiara clicked off the call.

As hurt as she was, she at least owed Evan a call to say goodbye, didn't she? She stared at her phone screen, debating calling him to do just that when the screen started glitching. The fall onto hard floor earlier must have taken some kind of toll. Instead of her usual wallpaper picture of the Grand York, various images and old photos from years ago started scrolling by one after another; snapshots that brought up memories of days long past. It finally stalled on a photo of her and her mother smiling at the camera in front of the doors of the Grand York Hotel that last Christmas they'd had together.

Did a dropped phone even glitch like that? Or was some Christmas miracle trying to send her a message?

Chiara gave her head a brisk shake. Now she was just being fanciful and silly. Her phone was back to its normal screen when she looked at it again.

Her imagination had to be playing tricks on her.

CHAPTER FIFTEEN

HE WAS TOO LATE. Evan stared at the screen on his tablet and bit out a vicious curse. All flights were grounded. No aircraft would be flying in or out for the next several hours. He'd missed her. Chiara was gone. All because he'd been too blind and scared to realize how lucky he was to have ever found her.

As if to match his mood, a torrent of snow seemed to suddenly fall from the sky, accompanied by a sharp wind that shook the car. Evan leaned over the divider to tell the driver to pull over as soon as he could. There was no way the man could see more than a foot in front of him with the thick snow that seemed to have come out of nowhere.

The other man obliged with a grateful word of thanks. Great. Now he was stuck in a car in one of the lanes leading away from the airport.

Then he saw her.

Evan thought he had to be imagining it. That

the murky visibility was showing him what he wanted to see. But upon closer inspection, he had no doubt. A familiar figure stood up from a bench near the entrance and gathered two small bags sitting on the ground. Evan was out of the car and running to her side in a flash.

"Chiara."

She paused, frozen in place. Finally, she turned to face him and the emotion he saw in her eyes nearly had his knees buckling.

"Evan?"

He reached her in two strides and took both her hands in his. "Hello, sweetheart."

"I was about to call you."

Her words sounded like a sweet melody. The knowledge that she couldn't bring herself to leave without saying goodbye had hope blossoming in his chest. But he couldn't get ahead of himself. He had one heck of an apology to deliver. Followed by a fair amount of groveling.

"What are you doing here?" she asked, still clearly dazed.

"I had to come catch you before you left for the States."

She blinked up at him, thick snowflakes falling on her dark lashes and ruddy cheeks. "You did?"

He nodded once. "You left in such a hurry that you left a couple of things behind. I had to make sure you took them with you before you left."

"What things?"

He reached into his pocket and removed the item he'd made a quick stop to pick up on the way.

"An ornament."

Hand crafted out of the finest crystal, encrusted with colorful gems and platinum carvings. He smiled at her. "To replace the novelty prize you won that day at the *kaitenzushi*."

She huffed a laugh. "This is a bit more elegant than the tiny plastic toy I won." Gently, she lifted the glass globe to eye level. "It's beautiful, Evan. Thank you. But you didn't need to get me a parting gift."

He shrugged. "Maybe not. I also wanted to give you this," he said, holding out the engagement ring.

She immediately shook her head, took a tiny step, backing away from him. "I can't. I didn't mind wearing it temporarily, but a woman shouldn't accept an engagement ring as her own unless she's actually getting engaged."

He reached for her, taking her hand in his. "I agree. That's why I'm giving it back to you." Despite the wet snow, Evan had no hesitation in doing what he did next. Dropping to one knee, he slipped the ring back on her finger. "No pretending this time."

Her jaw dropped. She blinked once, then again. Her eyes questioningly narrowing at him. "Evan? I…uh… I don't know what to say."

"Say yes."

She squeezed her eyes shut. "I need to know this is what you really want, Evan. Last night—"

He cut her off before she could say more. Standing back up, he pulled her closer. "Last night I was being a ridiculous, thoughtless fool. I know that now."

"You do?"

He nodded at her. "Chiara, you're the missing piece I never knew I needed in my life."

"I am?"

He chuckled. "Yes! You give away money that you desperately need so that someone you barely know can go see her injured boyfriend. You stick up for a man you just met to his imposing, hypercritical mother. You are absolutely extraordinary. You don't even know how special you are. It's no wonder I've fallen hopelessly in love with you."

She cupped a hand to her mouth. "Oh, Evan. I've fallen in love with you, too." Her eyes were glistening as she admitted what he'd known deep in his soul for days now. And full of love. For him. He winced inside to think he might have let someone who actually loved him walk out of his life for good. Some lucky twist of fate had saved him from that terrible mistake. For that, he'd be forever grateful. And he'd do whatever it took to make it up to her, for the way he'd behaved last night and all the things he'd said.

If she would only give him the chance.

Chiara still wasn't sure if she was, in fact, imagining things. It had all started with the strange scrolling pictures on her phone, some she hadn't even called up in ages. Then masses of snow had fallen from above as the skies opened up. And through the wall of white flakes, Evan Kim had somehow materialized and approached her. He stood before her now. Asking her to marry him.

It couldn't be real. Could it?

Until she figured it all out, Chiara reminded herself she had to be strong. She was holding her own, fighting the urge to throw herself into Evan's arms and admit how much she'd missed him, how despondent she'd felt when she thought they'd never see each other again. Even when he'd presented her with the handcrafted work of art ornament, she'd held strong. But the ring could very well lead to her undoing, to a complete shattering of her resolve. He'd slipped it back on her finger literally on bended knee.

But it behooved her to remain cautions and guard her heart. Because to lose Evan Kim twice in one lifetime would absolutely crush that said heart permanently and beyond repair.

"But what made you change your mind?" she asked, adding silently, *And how do I know you won't change it again?*

"The thought of going back home without you had me rethinking everything." He paused to take a deep breath. "I came to a realization."

"What was that?"

"I've been on my own most of my life, but you leaving was the first time I've ever *felt* alone. Even the new business deal didn't matter anymore." He stepped closer, gripped her hand tighter in his. "All that mattered was finding you. And never letting you out of my sight again."

Chiara had to remind herself to breathe. He was certainly saying everything she wanted to hear. How in the world was she supposed to resist such strong words of endearment? He was saying he loved her. She believed him with every fiber of her being. She loved him just as much. The last of her self-control crumbled to dust.

Flinging herself into his arms, she nestled against his chest, reveling in the sensation of being held by him again.

She sniffled, found a way to make her mouth work somehow. "I guess if I have to miss Christmas in Vermont, I'm glad I'll be able to at least spend it here with you."

Tilting her chin up with his finger, he narrowed his eyes at her. "Miss Christmas at home? Why on earth would I allow you to do that?"

She pointed to the sky, then motioned to the flakes that had already formed a thick layer of white over their hair and shoulders. And every other surface for that matter. "In case you haven't noticed, we're in the middle of a massive snowstorm. Every flight out of this place has been grounded for the foreseeable future."

"Maybe those flights have been grounded indefinitely, but I have a private jet that can be at your service as soon as the snow lightens and we get clearance."

"We?"

"I'd love to accompany you to Vermont. That's if the invitation still stands."

"You want to come home with me?"

"If you'll still have me. But I know I have no right to ask. I can come meet them later at some other time. Whatever you'd prefer."

Another sniffle escaped her. "I'd prefer it very much if you would come to Vermont with me to meet my father and brother. So that I can introduce them to the man I plan to marry."

As the thick white snowflakes fell like magical pixie dust around them, his answer was to gather her in his arms and claim her mouth the way she'd so badly wanted him to since he'd found her again.

"We should be landing in just a few minutes." Evan gave Chiara's hand a gentle squeeze. He couldn't seem to stop touching her. His jet and pilot had been readied for takeoff as soon as they'd gotten clearance. Now, Evan was taking his fiancée—his real wife-to-be—back to her home for the holidays.

"I can't wait to get to the cottage." Excitement rang in Chiara's voice as she looked out the window as the aircraft began its final descent. Usually while flying, Evan would be spending the time in the air trying to get some work done. Now, instead, he was simply letting himself enjoy the downtime. Then again, now that he had her back, he wanted to enjoy every moment he was in Chiara's company.

What a fool he'd been to think he could simply give that up after experiencing it. If it weren't for Chiara, he'd be heading back to his penthouse in Bali right now. By himself. The most enticing part of his days back home would be going over spreadsheets and debugging code.

The worst of it was he would have never even known all that he was missing out on.

Chiara continued, "They probably cut down the Christmas tree already. We do that every year. But maybe you and I can take a walk to the woods behind the cottage, find another smaller tree to call our own. There've been plenty of years where we had two trees. Did I tell you that already?"

Evan chuckled. She most certainly had. "You might have mentioned it once or twice. But I want to hear it all again. Tell me more."

"Really?"

He nodded. "Absolutely."

The smile she sent his way was like a shot of serotonin straight into his core. He'd never get enough of her smiling at him, was looking forward to indulging in that smile every day for the rest of his life.

Chiara went on. "Well, we spend the evening watching classic holiday movies—Marco and I share the same favorites—with Christmas cookies, of course. It's not as glamorous as what you're used to in an international hot spot city like Singapore or Bali but—"

She stopped mid-sentence, then laughed softly. "I'm probably boring you, aren't I? You're just being sweet, pretending to be interested in all the ways we Pearsons spend Christmas."

He had to laugh at that assessment. When in his lifetime had he ever been described as sweet? He couldn't think of one example. "You could never bore me, sweetheart." The weeks they'd spent together since he'd met could be described as anything but boring. In fact, Evan had had no idea what a drab and flat life he'd been leading until she came along. She'd awoken a part of him he'd forgotten had even existed. A part he'd shut down after losing his ahma when he was eleven years old. The part that knew how to love.

He had Chiara to thank for bringing that part of him back to life.

"I'm just so excited to finally be going home," she continued. "And to be able to share it all with you."

He leaned over the seat to kiss her softly on the cheek. "For the record, I'm excited to be going home with you, too."

She had no idea how true a statement that was. Thanks to Chiara, for the first time in his life, he'd be spending the holidays as part of a true family.

* * * * *

*Look out for the next story in the
A Five-Star Family Reunion trilogy,
One-Night Baby to Christmas Proposal
by Susan Meier, coming soon!*

*And if you enjoyed this story,
check out these other great reads
from Nina Singh*

Whisked into the Billionaire's World
Around the World with the Millionaire
From Wedding Fling to Baby Surprise

All available now!